Last Warriors on the Llano

Other Avalon Books by Howard Pelham

THE LAW OF SAN LUIS WASH
RAID AT BLACK PERSIMMON BLUFF
BADMEN OF THE BITTERROOTS
LAND WITH NO LAW
THE GALLOWS GANG
OUTLAW MOUNTAIN AMBUSH
QUEST FOR APACHE GOLD
TIRED GUN
TWELVE WAGONS WEST

LAST WARRIORS on the LLANO

Howard Pelham

AVALON BOOKS
THOMAS BOUREGY AND COMPANY, INC.
401 LAFAYETTE STREET
NEW YORK, NEW YORK 10003

24328051
S369

PRINTED IN THE UNITED STATES OF AMERICA
ON ACID-FREE PAPER
BY HADDON CRAFTSMEN, SCRANTON, PENNSYLVANIA

W
Cop. 1

Chapter One

Texas Ranger Cody Carson was busy packing a few things for his trip. He had three weeks of leave coming, and he badly wanted to get away before some kind of trouble erupted to delay him, as it already had a couple of times. He hadn't made any elaborate plans, but he generally knew what he would do during the time off.

He would take a leisurely ride north to Denver, hunting his food along the way and enjoying his time alone. At the end of the ride he would take a few days to enjoy the pleasures of that high-altitude town he had heard so much about. And when his money ran low, he and the steel-dust mare, his favorite mount, would hop a train home.

He hung the saddlebags over a shoulder and picked up a small war bag in which he carried a spare suit of clothes a little finer than the

1

denim shirt and jeans he wore, and a few other items, such as spare matches, extra salt, and plenty of ground coffee. He eyed the bedroll he had just tied off and the Winchester carbine in the corner of the cabin. His six-gun, a rust-pitted old Colt .45, the only six-gun he had ever owned, hung on the back of a chair. Deciding that he couldn't comfortably manage both the bedroll and the guns, he grabbed the bedroll and left the cabin.

A half mile away was Mobeetie, headquarters of the detachment of Rangers. A few tails of smoke curled up from buildings as women lit fires to cook midday meals. Mobeetie was a tough little town in the Texas Panhandle, and in its short history, it had known its share of trouble. Cody was looking forward to being free of the familiar dusty street and the eight hundred or so citizens who called it home, though there were certainly some good people in the town. The steeldust mare in the corral gave Cody her personal greeting as he crossed the yard.

Cody was an impressive figure of a man. He was six-two and weighed a hundred and eighty pounds. He had the lean hips and narrow waist of a broncobuster and the broad shoulders of a man used to lifting heavy weights. Even beneath the slight load he now carried, his muscles rippled under the denim shirt, and there was a general impression of taut physical power.

His appearance wasn't one that would have been called handsome. His light-brown hair had an unruly curl and always looked a little ragged. And his brows, darker than his hair, were thick and bushy. His eyes were small placid lakes of blue, and though much admired by women, their sharp gaze made men uneasy. High cheekbones and swarthy skin spoke of some Cherokee ancestry. His lips were firm and straight, and his white teeth flashed disarmingly when he smiled.

Cody saddled the mare and tied the bedroll and war bag on behind. Leading the mare, he crossed the yard again. He stopped before the cabin, ground-reined the mare, and entered the cabin to get the guns. When he came out, he had strapped on the holstered Colt and tied it down. He carried the rifle in his hand, and he shoved it securely into the boot attached to the mare's saddle.

Though Cody had a reputation with guns, he wasn't known as a quick-draw artist. Instead, he was known as a dead shot, and in a face-off, of which he had had many as a Ranger, he was known to be a dangerous man. Getting off the first shot wasn't what concerned him, but getting off the one that *counted* did. His motto, which he had never voiced aloud, was, "better be sure than fast." Thus far, that practice had paid off.

Hearing the sound of pounding hooves, Cody turned and looked toward town. As he recognized the rider, his spirits sank. Bart Stevens, a fellow Ranger, was crossing the flat meadow between the cabin and Mobeetie at a furious pace. Afraid of what Bart's ride portended, Cody thought of vaulting into the saddle and making a race of it. But he remained standing beside the mare and before the cabin, releasing his rising frustration in a silent oath.

Bart stopped before Cody and stepped down with a relieved look on his face. "By gandy, Cody, I'm glad I caught you," he said, wiping at his sweating face with a work-roughened palm. "The captain said he'd take a patch off my hide if I didn't get out here before you rode out."

Captain Tom Jones, who commanded the detachment of Rangers at Mobeetie, was a rugged, rough-edged Texan whose service with the Rangers went all the way back to the war with Mexico for independence. He had been a sprout then, but he had distinguished himself, as he had continued to do in his long service as a Texas lawman. Men like Tom Jones symbolized what the Rangers had come to stand for in Texas. No job was too tough for them to tackle, and odds were never figured. A single Ranger had been known to whip the most lawless Texas county into shape, and what those legendary Rangers had done was what Tom Jones expected his own men to accomplish. As a result, he generally inspired men to give more than they thought they had in them.

"I don't suppose you'd ride back in and just say you didn't get out here in time to stop me?" Cody asked.

"I wish I had the nerve, Cody. Anyhow, I think this might be something big. Came in a dispatch on the stage from the south. The captain got all worked up. Said for me to ride out here and get you, and I'd better not come back without you."

"Did he say what it was about?"

"No, he didn't. You know how closemouthed the captain is. He just told me to ride out here and fetch you in, and that I'd better get here before you rode out, which, thank goodness, I did."

For a moment Cody considered ignoring the summons. He hadn't had any real time off in over a year and he had been looking forward to getting away. But he knew Captain Jones. If he really wanted Cody, the hard-nosed old Ranger was capable of riding out and tracking him down.

"You'd better ride in and talk to him," Bart said as if he were reading the older Ranger's mind. Bart had been a Ranger for only six months, and he was uneasy in the position he was in. The captain had actually ordered him to bring Carson in—even if he had to track him down. Sensing Cody's thoughts, Bart wondered what would happen if Cody tried to ride off, and he, Bart, tried to carry out the order. His ruddy young face darkened nervously at the prospects.

Cody saw the young Ranger's discomfiture, and he smiled. "It's all right, Bart. I ain't gonna make you hog-tie me and carry me in across my horse."

"I don't think I could manage that, Cody, even if I had the nerve to try. Maybe whatever the captain wants won't take long."

"We'll see," Cody said.

Cody swung astride the mare, and the two men rode for town.

Captain Jones eyed Cody across the desk with a piercing look. "Carson," he said, "I'm sorry to call you in like this, but when you get this job done, you can add a few more days to your leave. Where were you going? Denver, wasn't it?"

"Yes, sir, I was riding up to Denver."

"Well, Denver will still be waiting when you get back."

"What is this job, Captain?" Cody asked with a wry smile. That was always the captain's answer: "Add a few more days when you finish the job." If he took all those days that the captain had offered at such times, he might have had a full year of paid leave.

"You're to ride down to Palo Duro Canyon and investigate the murder of a rancher and the disappearance of his family. The man's name was Amos Tate and his ranch is located in an extension of the big canyon called Beaver Creek. You've ridden that area a time or two. Would you happen to have known the man and his family?"

"No, sir," Cody replied. "You got any idea who killed him and why, Captain? Or what happened to the family?" Remembering what Bart Stevens had said about a dispatch from the south, and now seeing the papers on the Captain's desk, Cody nodded at them.

"That's an account written out and sent up to me by Charles Goodnight. Wordy as all get-out and not worth a hoot. Goodnight may know something about grabbing land and cattle, but he don't know beans about collecting information about a crime. He says you're to contact him when you get down there, if there happens to be anything he can do."

Charles Goodnight was already a legend in the Southwest. He was also a cattle king in the Panhandle. He had early on staked out a claim to the whole of Palo Duro Canyon. Thus far he had made that claim stick.

"Then you don't have any idea what happened down there," Cody said.

"No, I don't. Could be the work of any number of varmints. As you well know, there are plenty of outlaw gangs along the cattle trails that could have carried out a raid, and none of them are above grabbing a woman when they ride out."

"You mean Tate's wife?" Cody asked.

"Wasn't his wife. His wife has been dead for years, according to Goodnight."

"But you said his family had disappeared."

"A daughter and a son. The girl is nineteen or twenty, the boy ten or eleven. Poor girl, she may be dead by now . . . probably better off if she is. Don't know about the boy. I just can't figure what outlaws would want with a boy."

"You said this might be the work of any number of gangs. Who else were you thinking of, Captain?" Cody asked.

"Goodnight mentions a raid by comancheros on a small ranch to the east of the Palo Duro."

"Comancheros? I thought they disappeared when the Comanches were defeated by the Army and hauled north to the reservation near Fort Sill, which dried up their trade with the Indians. All that was twenty years ago. You reckon they've turned from traders into raiders and come back again?"

"They were never above doing some raiding on their own, but you were just a shavetail then. Maybe you don't remember."

"I remember the one the Army hanged."

"You mean old José Tofoya?"

"That's the one. A few soldiers unhitched his mules from the wagon and hanged him from the wagon tongue because there wasn't a handy tree."

"He was as mean as a rattlesnake, that one was," Captain Jones muttered. "Deserved to have his neck stretched. Well, he had a son named Juan, and Goodnight says the son is probably responsible for the raid to the east of Palo Duro. Maybe he and his bunch made the Tate raid as well. That's what you're going down there to find out."

"Yes, sir."

"Bring that girl and boy back . . . if they're still alive."

"Yes, sir, I'll do my best."

"Reckon you're already saddled and ready to ride," Jones continued. "Need any more supplies?"

"Guess I better take a few more. Hunting ain't as good to the south as it is between here and Denver."

"Draw what you need from the mercantile, then."

"Yes, sir."

Having been dismissed, Cody rose and walked to the door. As he turned the knob, the captain spoke again:

"Almost forgot. There's a cowhand you'll want to talk to, man by the name of Shorty Rhodes. According to Goodnight, Rhodes and Tate have a long history together. Tate was in command of a cavalry company during the Comanche War, and Rhodes was a sergeant under his command. Seems that the two hit it off, and Rhodes has been riding for Tate since they left the Army. He'll be able to give you some details about the missing girl and boy."

"Where was Rhodes when the raid happened?" Cody asked.

"Helping out on a cattle drive. Goodnight lets the smaller ranches add to his drives, but they have to send a man along to help out. Rhodes was returning from a drive to Kansas when the ranch was hit."

"If he goes so far back, maybe he's got an interest in the ranch."

"As a matter of fact, he has," the captain said. "Goodnight mentions that."

"Convenient . . . him being away," Cody added. "Maybe he got greedy and wanted it all."

"You'd suspect your own mama if she was near the scene of the crime," Jones said. "But it won't hurt for you to investigate this gent. You can make up your mind about him once you're on the scene. Now get out of here."

Cody was at the door when the captain spoke again: "One more thing, Carson."

"Yes, sir."

"Good luck, Ranger. Take care of yourself."

Cody was touched. Tom Jones seldom expressed such sentiments, and those parting words were an enormous departure for him. *Maybe the old boy's softening up a little,* Cody thought.

As he left the building, he wondered how long it would take to reach Palo Duro Canyon, and he decided he could make the ride in six or seven days and not push his mount too hard. Well, he wasn't headed for Denver, but he would have a long and solitary ride, anyway.

Chapter Two

Cody Carson sat his mount on the rim of the Palo Duro and stared into its depth . . . an abyss with a sudden drop of about fifteen hundred feet. He had passed through the huge canyon before, but the awesome grandeur of the steep cliffs and the fissure gouged from the earth by the forces of nature always left him in awe.

He peered into the canyon, and the features on the canyon floor seemed to have been executed on some miniaturized scale. There were rounded, gently rolling hillocks dotted with piñon and cactus. A line of cottonwood and willow, with a few pines mixed in, bordered a small river whose bed meandered through the mounds, seeking out the low ground. A wind sprang up as Cody watched, and it rippled through the rich buffalo grass that carpeted the ground along the river not covered by the trees. As the leaves of

13

the cottonwoods and willows were stirred by the wind, their silvery undersides flashed sunlit winks up at Cody.

"Looks mighty peaceful right now, don't it, hoss?" he muttered to the steeldust. Then he sent the horse south again, following the rim of the canyon.

Not too far ahead was a way down, an ancient path that wound through deeply eroded slits in the cliff that had been eaten out by centuries of rain. Sometimes the passage was no more than a few feet wide. Its rocky floor was worn smooth and slick from the padded hooves of animals making their way up and down. Once, Cody had almost collided with a grizzly who had decided to leave the canyon at the same time that Cody was going down. Fortunately, there had been space enough for him to turn his mount around and skedaddle back up. He had stood a hundred yards away and watched the big bear ramble across the plains before he entered the passage again. A little concerned about what he might meet coming up, Cody eased the steeldust into the opening and began the trip down.

He made it uneventfully, and once on the floor of the canyon, he sent the steeldust straight for the banks of the river and into the shade of the cottonwoods that towered above the gently coursing flow. Stepping down, he allowed the horse to drink. Then he removed the hackamore and gently slapped the mare on her rump, a signal that she was free to wander from the shade and graze awhile.

Easing down to his belly, Cody took a deep drink too. The water was sweet, pure, and cool, and he slapped some onto his face before he pushed himself up. The mare was grazing a few steps away, and he walked over to her, opened a saddlebag, and took out some jerky. Back in the shade again, he sat with his back to the bole of a cottonwood and chewed on the meat. Glancing at the sun overhead, he decided that the time was an hour or so past noon, which meant that he'd make the Tate ranch before dark. To make sure, he took out a map he had roughly sketched to check again the location of Beaver Creek Canyon. Figuring that his estimate was correct, he leaned his head against the cottonwood and stared out across the canyon, his eyes finally traveling up the tall cliff of the canyon's western wall.

He knew something of the history of the Palo Duro. The Quahadi Comanches had used it as their winter home. Each year before the blizzards swept in from the north and wreaked havoc on the plains with several feet of snow and freezing cold, the Quahadi moved into the Palo Duro. While the world above shivered, the

Quahadi prospered, protected by the high canyon walls from the miseries of winter. While their prized horses grazed the protected hay, the Quahadi hunters sought out the buffalo that, using the same good judgment of the Quahadi, had sought shelter from the cold.

Overhead, an eagle spotted its prey and swooped low. It disappeared for an instant behind one of the hillocks, and when it came up again, a jackrabbit struggled in its grip. Then the eagle disappeared to the north. For a moment there was silence along the stream. Then, with the danger gone, the small birds in the trees along the river began their chatter again. High overhead, puffy clouds drifted east and seemed to peer into the canyon as they passed aloft. *What a paradise the Quahadi must have thought the canyon to be!* Cody mused. He wondered why they hadn't spent all their days here instead of wandering the Staked Plains above during spring, summer, and fall.

There were ample signs that others used the canyon now. The riverbank was pitted by the sharp hooves of Texas longhorns. Their dung dotted the shade in which Cody sat, and there was sign of their grazing. Pushing himself up, he crossed to the mare, slipped her nose back into the hackamore, tightened the cinch he had loosened earlier, and climbed into the saddle.

He gave the mare the signal to move out and she responded with some spirit.

A couple of hours later Cody pulled up before the mouth of a small, narrow canyon. A crude sign beside the trail that led in told him he had reached his destination. As he turned the mare into the canyon, he noticed the fresh sign where cattle had been driven out.

He smelled smoke at once, but a twist in the canyon blocked his view of what might be burning up ahead. A few minutes later he rounded the curve and saw what remained of the smoking ruins of a ranch house. Some smoke still curled up from the blackened remains. A cottonwood nearby had turned brown from the heat, and a wide swath of burned grass surrounded the rectangular remains. Oddly, the barn and surrounding corral remained intact in the middle of the burned grass.

Cody pulled up before the smoldering ashes and stepped down. The heat was still sufficient to keep him back several yards, and he could only stand and peer into the crumbled remains of the house. He spotted the cast-iron stove in the area that must have been the kitchen, and there were also pots and pans. He saw or smelled nothing suggesting that Shorty Rhodes might have died in the fire.

Stepping back from the hot ashes, Cody surveyed the surrounding canyon, a small version of the bigger canyon beyond. A small creek split its middle, and there was the accompanying line of trees. On each side the canyon walls rose high and sheer.

But there was a difference. The sounds of nature had echoed along the big canyon. There had been the sound of the sweeping wind through the grass and trees, and the chatter of songbirds, and the cry of the eagle as it swept away with the rabbit. Here there was profound silence, as if whatever had happened here had muted even nature. Cody studied the trees along the stream, the canyon walls, and the inner depths of the canyon for the cause of the silence, but he could detect no threat of any kind. A slight shiver, of which he was ashamed, quivered along his spine.

Again he wondered about Shorty Rhodes. Was the man out there somewhere and watching the place? Was the silence due to his presence? If he was around, why didn't he come out and make his presence known? Turning about, Cody began to circle the burning ruin, looking for a clue to what had happened.

There was sign that riders had recently circled the house, and he found some fresh boot prints as well. Maybe they were Shorty Rhodes's, but if they weren't, there was now no way to identify who had walked there. Then he spotted a spent shell. Picking it up, he decided it had come from some kind of a .44-caliber weapon. He found others as he rounded what had been the corner of the house.

Then he saw the body . . . that of a man. It lay in the grass directly opposite what must have been the back door of the house. There were some deeper boot marks, and Cody decided that whoever it was had been trying to flee.

The body lay sprawled faceup, his arms and legs spread-eagled and tied to stakes. A fire had been built beneath his legs. The flames had burned the man's clothes away, and the flesh of his legs had been viciously burned. Cody felt a twist of anger in his gut that anyone could do such a thing to a fellow human being.

He knew that the man had to be dead, but he decided to check and make sure. When he placed a hand gingerly over the heart, he was amazed to feel a faint beat. Then the man's eyelids fluttered weakly and his head turned slightly. Cody felt sure he had found Shorty Rhodes. Touching the man's chest, he said, "Rhodes? Shorty Rhodes?"

The man's eyes opened just a slit, and he whispered, "If you ain't one of them, who are you?"

"Carson of the Texas Rangers. You're Shorty Rhodes, aren't you?"

The man gave a weak nod.

"Can you tell me what happened here?"

"You got some water?"

Feeling a bit ashamed that he hadn't thought of water himself, Cody whistled for the mare and she circled and came to him. Cody took the canteen from the saddle, unscrewed the cap, and gave Rhodes a drink after lifting his head gently. Beneath Rhodes was a drying puddle of blood, and the back of his clothes were soaked with blood too. The man's wounds were in his back, which indicated that he had been trying to get away, probably after the house had been fired.

Rhodes managed only a swallow or so, and when Cody lowered his head to the ground again, his eyes went shut. For a moment, Rhodes appeared to have breathed his last. Then, with his eyes still closed, he whispered very weakly, "Comancheros."

"Can you give me a name? A description?" Cody bent his ear to Rhodes's lips in order to better catch his reply.

"Tofoya!" he cried, and as he spoke the name, he seemed to summon up more strength.

"Juan Tofoya?" Cody asked, remembering the comanchero family that the captain had mentioned.

"Yeah," Rhodes replied, and he seemed surprised that Cody would know the name.

"Did the same bunch make the first raid and then come back again?" Cody asked, afraid that the wrangler had become too weak to talk any more.

"Yeah," came the faint answer.

"How do you know? You weren't here during the first raid, were you?"

"I heard them talking. They took the horses the first time. Then they came back for the cattle."

"Did you hear them say anything about the girl and the boy?"

"Mary and Brad?"

"Yes."

"They got 'em and they're still alive."

"Where are they? Did you hear anyone say?"

Rhodes didn't answer, and the hand Cody placed to his heart detected no beat this time. Rhodes was dead.

While Rhodes lived, Cody had concentrated on getting as many answers as he could. Now he had time to examine the little wrangler more closely. In addition to the shots to the back that had brought him down, there were signs of a beating.

Most gruesome, however, had been the torture. The smell of burnt flesh still drifted up

from where the small fire had burned beneath
the man's legs. How had he stood the pain and
continued to live? With the pain of the bullet
wounds to contend with, the agony from the fire
may have been only a distant ache. Pain was
just pain beyond a certain point. Hopefully, that
had been the way it was.

The torture told Cody the type of men he
would have to contend with if he ever caught up
with them, which he would, of course. His orders
were to rescue the woman and the boy if they
remained alive, and apparently they were. But
the sight and smell of Rhodes's burned flesh
made Cody vow not to let himself fall into Juan
Tofoya's hands.

Rhodes still lay spread-eagled upon the
ground and Cody unsheathed his bowie and slit
the ropes that bound him to the stakes. He would
give the little wrangler a decent burial before
he took up the trail of his killers.

The cattle trail led south, which surprised
Cody. Charles Goodnight's headquarters was
there, and there was no chance that the cattle,
which appeared to be well over a hundred head,
would get past Goodnight's men without someone spotting them and making an inquiry. That
could mean only one thing: Tofoya meant to

leave the canyon somewhere between Beaver Creek Canyon and Goodnight's headquarters.

Cody's knowledge of the Palo Duro was not complete, but he considered the various exits he knew of. There was only one between Goodnight's headquarters and Beaver Creek Canyon where the comancheros might be able to leave the big canyon with the herd—Wild Horse Pass.

How the pass had been formed no one knew. Folks speculated that some upheaval deep within the canyon wall had caused a cave-in. The crumbling cliff had formed a steep slope that animals on the llano used to reach the water. The most frequent users in numbers had been the herds of wild horses that once had roamed the vast and empty stretches of the Llano Estacado, and some of whom still inhabited the caprock plain.

Cody calculated that Tofoya had at least a day's start. The cattle would slow him down, but if the bandits were to be caught before they were deep into the desert of the llano, Cody could waste no time. Confident that the comancheros were headed for Wild Horse Pass, he left the cattle trail that tended to follow the curves and twists of the west wall of the Palo Duro and headed straight for the pass. As he rode, he was aware that daylight would soon be dwindling fast.

On the way to Wild Horse Pass, he rode past the entrance to Bone Canyon. The small box canyon received its grisly name after the last battle between the cavalry and the Comanches. The cavalry had surprised Quanah Parker's forces as they rested up in the depths of the Palo Duro.

During the battle that followed, the cavalry captured most of the Comanche horses, and the Comanches took refuge in the vast reaches of the llano. Without their horse reserves, they could no longer employ the hit-and-run tactics with which they had successfully fought the cavalry. Within the year, small bands began to straggle in and give themselves up, after which they were marched north to Indian Territory, where the reservation near Fort Sill had been set aside for them.

Colonel McKenzie had not been content just to capture the herds of horses. Fearful that the Comanches would return and steal their mounts, he ordered the horses driven into a small box canyon and shot.

The meat scavengers must have had quite a picnic during the following days as they picked the bones of more than two thousand slaughtered horses. Though Cody did not turn into the canyon on this day, he had paid a visit another time. The bleached bones of the horses still lit-tered the floor of the small canyon, a silent memorial to the slaughter. He had walked among the bones and envisioned how red the canyon floor must have run with blood on that fateful day. A lover of horses and respectful of their contribution to humanity, he had known that he could never have given such an order himself, regardless of the threat of theft by the Comanches.

The mare made good time, and an hour later, with some daylight still remaining, Cody pulled up at the foot of the slope known as Wild Horse Pass. As he had expected, cattle had recently been driven up the steep slope, and he studied the sign to convince himself that the numbers were about the same as the herd he had trailed from Beaver Creek Canyon. Then he sent his horse up the slope. When he topped out at the summit, he pulled up again.

The western llano stretched out before him, a rusty sea that had no end. A lonely silence hung over the infinite brown terrain, reminding Cody of the brooding quiet he had left behind in Beaver Creek Canyon. On the far horizon, a tint of blue formed a curtain that gradually faded out some distance above the horizon. The sun inched its way toward that mysterious tapestry as if to take a bite out of it. From behind that deep azure shade, low clouds, their bases threateningly black, drifted up and sailed toward Cody. When they passed between him and the lowering sun, ominous shadows crawled eastward over the brown rolling swells of the llano.

Cody knew something of the boundaries of the Llano Estacado. From Palo Duro Canyon it ran westward to the banks of the Pecos River, deep into New Mexico Territory. There was its eastern portion as well. Now settled by cattle barons, the caprock that was the llano reached deep into West Texas. From the Cherokee Outlet in the north, it ran to the Colorado River in Texas and circled the vast badlands north of the river.

The Apaches had once claimed the llano, but the Comanches, drifting steadily south, had driven the Apaches farther south, claiming the mostly desert region as their own. Then the whites had wrested it from the Comanches. During the Comanche wars, comancheros had come out of Mexico, crossed the desert, and traded with the Comanches, bringing, among other things, guns, ammunition, and rotgut whiskey. In return, they had received whatever the Comanches had to trade, which included white captive women who were sometimes ransomed back to their families. Others were taken deep into Mexico and sold as slaves.

From deep in the Palo Duro came the roar of a grizzly. A powerful and defiant sound, the snarling bellow seemed to climb the walls before it bounced back into the canyon once again. The steeldust trembled beneath Cody at the sound. She wanted the signal to move out, and Cody gave it to her.

A hot wind, carrying the smell of the desert upon it, brushed Cody's face as the mare got under way. Here was a land not only of hot wind but also of sun and solitude, and Cody had the feeling he was the first man ever upon it, though before him was the trail of the cattle pulling him into that desolation like a magnet.

But the llano wasn't featureless. Its plains were broken by a network of ravines and gorges, invisible till one was almost upon them. In these canyons were found the only streams known to exist in the llano. They were mostly tiny ribbons of water that oozed from beneath the walls of the gorges to provide a little moisture for the mesquite, cottonwoods, and buffalo grass that provided a haven for men with the courage, or lack of judgment, to venture into these wilds. They were little oases of life in an otherwise barren world.

From time to time the bandits had driven the cattle into a gorge for a drink. After each stop the sign became fresher, and Cody knew he was rapidly gaining though he was now riding into a brilliant sunset of burnt orange that gradually changed to blood red. Before the large rusty coin that was the sun was totally consumed by the darkening horizon, he descended into a deep ravine to spend the night.

He looked to the needs of the mare first, stripping her of her gear and rubbing her down. When she had cooled off some, he led her to the pitifully small pool to drink. The mare then took a good wallow, and Cody staked her on some of the sparse buffalo grass surrounding the pool. Only then did he see to his own needs.

Beneath an overhang he built a small fire from dry mesquite twigs, and when there were sufficient ashes to spread a little, he put some coffee on to boil. Next he dug out a frying pan and opened a can of beans. After dumping the beans into the pan, he whittled off some jerky into the beans for more flavor. Finally he set the frying pan on the ashes beside the coffeepot. The smells of burning mesquite, boiling coffee, and cooking beans soon permeated the ravine, which made Cody nervous, because they were a beacon for anyone riding the llano above. He was thankful he had taken a good look around before descending into the ravine for the night. Still, he took his supper off the fire as soon as it was hot, and after extinguishing the flames, he ate by the light of a few early stars that hung just above him.

When Cody had eaten his slim fare, he spread

his bedroll. After removing only his boots and then carefully placing the Winchester and the Colt within reach of his hand, he crawled into the blankets to sleep. His bones were weary from his long ride that day. Even so, sleep was slow to come, and he lay and stared up at the thickening stars through the slit above him. Their increased numbers seemed to extend their distance from Earth.

A hoot owl in a cottonwood objected to his presence in the ravine. As the mare grazed, the soft sound of pulled grass was as reassuring as the talk of a friend. That sound in the night was the lullaby of trail-weary cowboys. And finally Cody slept.

A snort from the mare awoke Cody. He had no idea of how long he had slept, and he reached out a hand to feel the ashes from his fire. They were cold. Raising himself up, he peered at the mare.

A faint moon lit the ravine and he could see her. She faced the trail that led down into the ravine. Her ears were thrown forward and she was about to give a second warning. Cody spoke a reassuring warning and threw the blankets aside. He reached for the six-gun and strapped it on. Next he shook out his boots, pulled them on, grabbed the rifle, and went to stand by the mare's head.

Something or someone dislodged a rock at the top of the trail, and Cody spoke to the mare again. He felt as though he needed some reassurance of his own, for he was jittery as he sought to penetrate the shadowy darkness of the trail. Had Tofoya somehow guessed he was back there and sent someone to scout his backtrail? Cody hated to think he had been that careless, but he also knew he was following a savvy bunch.

There was the clatter of several horses as the party descended into the gorge. Cody yanked the stakes from the ground and moved deeper into the cottonwoods and some underbrush. Then the riders emerged from the high banks siding the trail and into the moonlight surrounding the pool. Cody thought that he had to be seeing things, because the sight was so uncommon.

They were Indians, and not the tame Indians he had become accustomed to seeing during his infrequent trips into Indian Territory. Called sneeringly "blanket Indians" by whites, those other Indians were beaten and whipped. They were now dependent on government handouts, and they showed their defeat in the prideless way they sat their scrawny ponies. Their weary eyes had been filled with hate and loathing when they looked on Cody.

These five Indians were different, even in the way they eased in their mounts to drink from the small pool while the moonlight reflected off the water and lit their faces. Cody's first thought was that they were Apaches, for Apaches were still running wild to the west. But as his eyes grew accustomed to the darkness and he could more clearly make out their features, he knew better. What he was looking at was a small war party of Comanches.

Comanches! But where had they come from? No Comanches had raided around Palo Duro Canyon in over twenty years, not since they had been marched north after their surrender.

Their appearance at the little pool was one of magnificent wildness. The pale moon glistened off greased, muscular bodies. Their only garment was a loincloth, and their feet and lower legs were encased in knee-length moccasins. Headbands kept their long black hair from their faces, and each wore a single feather in the band.

War paint streaked their faces ... white lines shadowed underneath with black. The marks reached from the corners of their eyes into their temples, and there were strips on their cheeks and from the corners of the mouth. The moonlight glinted off the white paint and emphasized the savage look.

Each carried what appeared to be new Winchesters, but there were other weapons. Quivers of arrows were strapped over their shoulders and rested at their backs. Each carried a full-length war bow as well. The bows and arrows didn't surprise Cody. He had heard many Indians tell of carrying their native weapons even after they learned to use the white man's guns. They were silent killers, to be used in surprise attacks.

As Cody took note of each of the five warriors, he became aware of a peculiar, surprising thing. With the exception of a single warrior, they were all very old; so old, in fact, that even in the dimness, Cody could see the wrinkles on their faces, and he could see age in their slumped backs and hanging muscles.

The exception was the warrior nearest Cody. He was a stalwart-looking man with a thick neck, broad shoulders, and powerful arms, the muscles of which rippled as he flicked the rein that reached to the halter on his mount. Suddenly, he slipped from his mount to drink. As he stretched facedown over the water, Cody took in the narrow waist and hips of the horseman. And there was the slight bow between the stretched legs that reminded him of old cowboys when they walked.

The others followed the young warrior's example and got down to drink. Then they remounted and seemed about to leave, and Cody breathed a sigh of relief. But one of them reined his horse beneath the overhang and sat staring down at Cody's gear and bedroll. He spoke gruffly to the others, words Cody couldn't understand, but whose meaning he could guess, and they gathered about him. The young warrior slid from his mount and began to poke among Cody's things.

Cody had to make a move. All his supplies were there, and he could resupply only back at the Goodnight ranch, a long ride away. He would lose days, and the thought made him a little desperate.

"Any of you savvy English?" he asked, stepping from the shadows. He did not draw the Colt, and he purposely kept the barrel of the rifle pointed at the ground.

The Indians froze. They were like statues in the moonlight. The first moments passed, and they made no move to bring their rifles to cover him. Then the young warrior, acting more and more like the leader, spoke softly, his words still unintelligible to Cody. But they seemed to carry a warning to the other four.

"Anybody speak English?" Cody asked again.

"*I* speak the white man's words," the young

warrior replied. Actually, he was not all that young. He just seemed young by comparison to the other four men.

Cody was struck by the words spoken in English, maybe as good as his own, but he wasn't about to spend time asking where the leader of a Comanche war party had picked up such good English. At any moment, unless he took the initiative to keep it from happening, one of those Indians might start shooting. He might get one or two, but they were certain to get him before the shooting stopped.

"I ain't looking for trouble," he said, trying to show none of his nervousness in his voice, "but those are my things there. I sure wouldn't take to losing them."

The young warrior, who had crouched beside Cody's saddle all the while, now rose slowly. Turning to the other Indians, he spoke something to them in their own language. The four old warriors appeared to relax a little.

"I hope you didn't tell them something you can't tell me," Cody said.

"I told them you're not one of the white men we're looking for," the young warrior said.

"Don't suppose it would do me any good to ask you who it is you're looking for?"

The Indian didn't answer. Then, with deliberate ease, he walked to his mount, grabbed a handful of mane, and in a single fluid motion swung himself up. He spoke again to the others. Then the little war party turned their mounts about, giving Cody a view of their backs. In an exhibition of cool courage, they rode up the trail and out of the ravine.

After the passage of several minutes, Cody brought the mare from the brush and staked her once more on the grass. Then he sat with his back to the cliff beneath the overhang and tried to sort out what he had just seen. There was no doubt that they were Comanches. He hadn't seen a party decked out for war in a long time, but these were unmistakable. But what were they up to, and where had they come from?

Cody stayed on guard till he saw pink gradually climb the eastern sky. Then, with an eye on the trail leading into the gorge, he built another small fire and boiled coffee and cooked his breakfast. When he was finished, he cleaned his cooking utensils and repacked everything. Then he led in the mare and saddled her. A few minutes later he rode cautiously out of the ravine. The llano was as flat and featureless as it had seemed the day before. Nowhere was there any sign of the Indians. With some relief, he picked up the cattle trail and headed west. Interestingly enough, so had the Indians, because the unshod prints of their ponies were clearly visible over the cattle sign.

The Comanche war party had brought a strange new twist to the situation. Recalling the younger Indian's comment, Cody wondered if the warriors were out to engage the bandits. If that were the case, he might use a clash between them to his own advantage. If the Indians reached the place where Mary Tate and the boy were being held, Cody might use the distraction of a fight to sneak in and free the captives. Even if it happened earlier, maybe he could get his hands on a prisoner and make him talk.

The fate of Mary Tate had been on Cody's mind since Mobeetie. She was in his mind even stronger now, almost as if she were someone known to him, whereas before he reached the Palo Duro she had been nothing more than a name. But, somehow, she now seemed closer, as though his having been at her home in Beaver Creek Canyon had made some kind of contact with her. He found himself wondering what she was like. Was she pretty or a woman as rough as a cob, as some frontier women turned out?

Would she be able to cope with being a captive and all that went with it? Some women could. Cody knew of women who had been held captive by Indians for years, and when they were rescued, they shook off those years as though what they had suffered hadn't happened at all. Others withered under the terror and the burden of what they were forced to do. They became less than human in their own eyes, and their captors tended to see them as they saw themselves. Thus the terror, even the torture, increased.

A strong woman stood a chance of surviving, however. Even the most depraved of men retained some speck of warmth in his soul for a woman who continued to respect herself. Cody found himself hoping that Mary Tate was a strong, clever woman.

As the day advanced, the heat increased, and the wind, which continued to blow from the southwest, reminded Cody of the first blast from an oven when it was opened. He felt its searing effect upon his face, and he noted that his perspiration was sucked away by the thirst of the wind for even the slightest moisture.

The vegetation about him withered too, the brown buffalo grass becoming more dwarfish and sparse. Mesquite gave way to greasewood, and the prickly pear seemed the only plant at home in a land so harsh.

A large lizard dashed across the trail in front of him. At least a foot long, the thing carried between his jaws a half-eaten snake. The dangling tail of the snake appeared to have two

buttons that would have eventually become rat-
tles. What kind of a land produced lizards that
hunted, killed, and ate rattlesnakes?

A distant crack—of a rifle?—caused Cody to
fling himself low on the mare's neck. Peering
anxiously to the south, from where the sound
had come, he saw a dust devil spring into being.
The churning, twisting dust spiraled higher and
higher, and soon grass and twigs were funneled
from its top. The gyrating column of dust weaved
its way eastward with the wind.

All the while Cody kept an eye on the distant
horizon. Since morning he had hoped to spot dust
from the cattle, and he found it strange that he
hadn't. He had often spotted, and from many
miles away, the dust tailing up from the Western Trail as the herds of longhorn were driven
north to Dodge. Those memories made the absence of dust ahead of him all the more strange.
By his calculations, the cattle had been only a
day ahead of him, and he was gaining. So where
was the herd? He pondered that question as he
rode.

About the middle of the afternoon, Cody came
upon some surprising sign. The Indians had split
up, two of them angling to the south and two to
the north, while a single set of unshod prints
continued to follow the cattle. He took a few
minutes to study the pattern of the dispersal,

which looked for all the world like some kind of encirclement.

Cody shook his head in bewilderment. What could the Comanches have in mind? For five of them, though well armed, to attack the dozen or so bandits driving the herd was comparable to a tabby cat's attacking a tiger. Were they actually capable of such foolhardiness?

Cody asked the steeldust for a spurt of speed. If the crazy Comanches were about to attack, he didn't want to miss out on taking a prisoner. Presumably, the captives were being held at some location farther ahead, and if he could nab one of the bandits and make him talk, he might bring his assignment to a close. After all, the captain had ordered him only to solve the mystery of Amos Tate's murder and bring the captives home. If he could take out a few of the bandits, preferably Juan Tofoya, well and good. But returning with Mary and Brad Tate was his chief concern.

The mare met the challenge, and the bare landscape of the desert flashed past. After a couple of hours of the faster pace, flecks of foam from the mare's mouth began to hit Cody damply in the face. The horse's flanks dripped sweat as well, and not even the thirsty wind was sufficient to keep it from falling to the dusty ground. Cody grew concerned that he might be sapping too much of the mare's strength. A spent horse in his situation could prove suicidal. What if someone up ahead spotted him, turned around, and gave chase? Still, he didn't slow down the steeldust.

As twilight approached, the shadows seemed to creep from the ground itself. The sunset promised to be as spectacular as yesterday's. But this sunset was a different matter. As the glaring bright light of this sun dimmed and reddened, there was something almost wrathful and irate about it.

Cody had never been one to read portents into natural occurrences, but the transformation above him made him uneasy. He knew that dust could work dramatic changes in light, and he thought of the dust from the herd that he still had to spot. Had the herd been driven along here earlier than he thought? Was it that dust, having worked itself high, that was causing the strange sky above him? Then the sun was gone and the livid colors began to fade.

He was searching for a campsite when he saw the bats. Not more than a couple of miles ahead, they seemed to boil up from the earth itself and scatter in the twilight like black leaves shaken from a limb. But Cody knew that bats didn't emerge from desert sand. They slept in dark recesses in the earth during the day, and at night they came out to feed on insects. Their presence suggested two things: There was a canyon with a cave up ahead, and if the bats were feeding on insects, there would be water. A bath from some trickling spring would be heaven-sent after the heat of the day, and Cody decided to push on.

Then he caught a whiff of mesquite smoke, and he pulled the mare up short.

He sat there a moment and tested the scent, and there was no mistaking it. The wind carrying the smoke smell came straight at him from the circling bats. Someone had a fire up there, most probably in the canyon with the bat cave. The mare, verifying Cody's judgment, gave a snort and cocked her ears in that direction. She smelled the smoke and probably had picked up some sound.

"I wish you could just talk a little, hoss," Cody said aloud. "Maybe you could tell me who's up there." But he knew. Apparently, the bandits had gone into an early camp, and maybe they had even been there all day. After all, they were returning from their second raid on the Beaver Creek ranch. No one had followed them the first time, and having killed Shorty Rhodes, they had no reason to believe that the second time would be different. Probably, they had decided to give themselves a day of rest.

Even as Cody sat there, darkness closed down as from a very thick fog. He gave the mare the signal to move out. Holding her down to a walk, he gave her plenty of time to sense what was ahead and to choose her footing carefully.

The pace was turtle slow, and the intense darkness gave Cody the feeling that he and the mare moved through total isolation, with nothing above or below or to either side. Then the mare came to an abrupt stop on her own.

Cody ran a reassuring hand along her neck to keep her silent and slipped from the saddle. After ground-reining the steeldust, he took a couple of careful steps forward, testing the ground before he put a foot down. Even then he almost stepped off into space and had to fight to maintain his balance. He returned to the mare and wondered what to do.

The smell of smoke was strong now, but it didn't come from the dark space Cody had almost stepped off into or he would have spotted some flames. Then from where? Maybe another canyon up ahead?

Then he heard an unexpected sound, the faint strumming of a guitar. He cocked his ear against the wind to better catch the sound, and he decided the music was Spanish. Somewhere up there and not too far away, the bandits were encamped.

Cody glanced into the sky. He found it curious that the stars were still not out. Was their absence caused by the same strange phenomenon that had so affected the sunset? He swore softly to himself. All he needed was just enough light to keep from stepping off a precipice and plunging to his death. But for the moment there was nothing he could do but wait. Drawing on the patience he had learned during numerous manhunts, he reached into a saddlebag and brought out some jerky. He settled himself on his haunches, put some of the dried beef between his teeth, and began to chew. Sooner or later the stars would eat through the overcast, or his eyes would become used to the heavy blanket of darkness.

Chapter Three

G radually, the sky began to brighten, and soon Cody could see his hand outstretched before him. Then he saw the faint glitter of the first star emerge from the dark overhead gloom. Whatever had kept the heavens shrouded in darkness was breaking up.

Cody took a long swig from his canteen to wash the jerky down. Back on his feet, he reached for the mare's rein and stepped to the rim where he had almost fallen. Many feet below he could see the outlines of some trees.

The rim meandered north and Cody followed it. After two hundred yards he reached a point where the canyon turned to the west, and he followed along till it finally turned south. Suddenly, the music sounded louder, and a minute later he saw the flicker of a campfire across what had to be a very broad expanse. The fire was about two miles away.

Cody stood and studied the situation a few minutes. The sky had gradually filled with stars, and he could make out the high walls of the canyon. The south wall made a wide, irregular circle, and he would have to travel a good three miles before he'd be able to peer down on the fire. His boots already seemed too tight on his feet from all the walking, and he tossed the rein oven the mare's head, stepped back, and climbed into the saddle. He let the horse choose her own pace, because of the uncertain footing. Thirty minutes later, Cody knelt on the edge of the canyon and peered down into the camp.

He saw the prisoner at once, but it was no white woman or boy. He looked down upon a half-naked Indian spread-eagled between four stakes, the position identical to the one from which he had cut Shorty Rhodes loose. The difference was that the Indian was still alive.

Not too far away four men sat about the campfire. A few yards out, but still within the circle of light, lay four others, covered with blankets, who appeared to be sleeping. Two others sat on the bank of a small pool some distance apart. They dangled their feet in the water, and the pale starlight glistened off their starkly white bodies.

From across the canyon came the sounds of the herd. Cody couldn't see the cattle, but their contented din suggested they had grazed well and had been allowed to water. Cody counted ten bandits, and there would be at least two others with the cattle.

One of the men at the fire rose and walked out into the darkness. A moment later he returned with an armful of branches. He threw a few onto the fire and put the others aside. Then he stood by the fire and stared at the outspread Indian. The bandit appeared to be smiling, but he was too far away for Cody to be sure. Then he reached down, took a burning branch from the fire, and crossed to where the Indian lay. He brandished the flame back and forth over the Indian's body, lowering it at times to within an inch of the bare flesh. Then the torch came to rest just above the Indian's groin. For the first time the Indian flinched. A belly guffaw floated up to where Cody crouched on the canyon rim.

Recalling the mutilation to which Shorty Rhodes had been subjected, Cody was sure that sooner or later the fire would be applied to the Indian. Bile rose in his throat at the memory, and at the thought that the same torture was about to be repeated on another man. He told himself that he hadn't been sent south to undertake the dangerous rescue of a wild Indian he didn't even know. His responsibility was to

Mary and Brad Tate, his own people. If he tried
to help the Indian and didn't come through it,
what would become of the Tates?

It was the strongest argument that Cody could
make, but it didn't ring true. He simply couldn't
sit and watch someone, even a savage Indian,
tortured and killed. But how was he to get the
Indian away from them? He thought that over
as he watched the bandit finish his sport with
the supine Indian and return to the fire. No plan
came to mind, but the first step, plan or no plan,
was to find a way into the canyon. Rising, he
turned to the mare, climbed back into the saddle,
and continued his circle of the canyon.

A half mile later he found the passage down,
but afraid there might be a guard posted, he slid
from the saddle and led the mare down the slope.
He took his time and made as little noise as he
could, but from time to time he slipped, and the
sound of his boots sliding on gravel seemed loud
enough to alarm the whole canyon. Once the
mare displaced a rock with a hoof. Cascading
down the slope, the stone sounded like rolling
thunder to Cody. Fortunately, the comancheros
felt secure. There was no guard on the passage,
and a few minutes later Cody stood on level
ground at the base of the slope beside the steeldust.

To his left the campfire flickered. From the

right and some distance away came the sounds of the herd. Slightly to the right of the campfire was the pool. In an irregular circle, the canyon walls rose dark and ominous. They would be prison walls if the exit slope were cut off.

Overhead the night sky suddenly lightened, and Cody saw that a pale moon had just broken through the overcast. More light was the last thing he needed. "Where were you when I needed you earlier?" he muttered to the moon.

Except for a few trees about the pool, the whole canyon floor was free of large vegetation. The only cover was a few large boulders scattered about. A possibility got Cody's attention. In the past, the cliff to his left, the one he had circled to find the passageway down, had caved in, depositing a line of loose shale at its base. He decided he might wind his way through that deposit and make his way very close to the campfire. Leading the mare into the fallen debris, Cody slipped the Winchester from its boot, ground-reined the mare, and began to work his way through the rocks.

He was within thirty yards of the fire when he pulled up behind a large boulder. He could hear the murmur of the men, and though he had some understanding of Spanish, he was too far away to catch what was being said.

Pushing his broad hat to the back of his neck, he eased up and draped himself on the rock and peered into the camp. The clothes of the four men near the fire varied hardly at all. They wore tattered sleeveless jackets and white cotton trousers, all of which were stained and grimed. Their feet were encased in leather sandals, and even at night they wore their Mexican sombreros pulled low on their heads. Each wore a bandolier of bullets slung from a shoulder and across his chest.

Several rifles were stacked on the fringe of the camp, but all the men wore heavy pistols at their waists. They were burly gents with hard faces and eyes. Cody wondered if he had ever looked upon a group more dangerous. Near one of them lay a guitar, and Cody had trouble envisioning the stout, bearded man strumming the instrument. His looks seemed more appropriate for bloodletting and murder than making music.

The two men who had sat naked on the bank of the pool now entered the camp. They were fully dressed, and their clothes as well as their features set them apart from the others. Instead of peasant dress, the two wore the clothes of caballeros. Though dusty and stained, their black shirts were of good material and form fitting. Brightly colored designs decorated the front of the shirts. The black trousers flared at the bottom, but they were short enough so that their fancy boots could be seen. Silver conchas flashed in the firelight from the sides of their pants and the bands of their broad, heavy hats.

They were handsome men, and their long dark hair glistened from dampness and fell about their shoulders. The firelight landed softly on the olive skin of their faces and made their dark eyes flash. When they passed near the Indian, they paused for a look at him. Cody could see their faces clearly, and their cold stares at the outstretched man made Cody shiver. He had a vision of these two standing by and enjoying the torture that Shorty Rhodes had been put through.

They had to be brothers, Cody knew. There was no other way to explain the similarity of their frigid, handsome features. One appeared to be a couple of years older than the other.

"Are you sure he's Red Wind, Juan?" the younger asked before they moved on.

"Couldn't be anyone else, Esteban. The rest of that band are all old men, except for the children. This is Red Wind. You can be sure of that."

"What are you going to do with him?"

"Kill him, of course."

"When?"

"First we'll let Jesus have some fun with him. The men always enjoy a little sport. It takes the place of women on a long raid like this. They won't spend so much time thinking about the blond woman back in the main camp."

"What are you going to do with her?" the brother called Esteban asked. "Will you keep her for yourself or sell her? She'd bring a handsome price in Mexico City."

"I don't know yet," Juan Tofoya replied.

"Well, you can't do both. Blondes bring big money. I say we sell her."

"You can say all you want to, my brother, as long as you remember I'm the one who will decide."

A hard stare passed between the two, and then Esteban dropped his eyes. "It shall be as you say, Juan," he said.

The older man slapped the younger on the back and laughed. "As long as you remember that, Esteban. Now I feel like a drink after that bath. Come, I've been saving a bottle of tequila."

The two passed on, but they didn't join the men at the fire. Instead, they crossed to two bedrolls that were set apart. Juan produced a bottle and he and his brother took long swigs. Then they sat down and lit long, thin cigars. They smoked and passed the bottle back and forth while the four men near the fire cast envious looks at them.

Cody now took a good long look at the Indian. There was no mistaking the supple, muscular form and the painted face. He was the man who had led the elderly warriors into the ravine where he had been camped. But how had they captured him? Then Cody recalled the lone set of prints that had continued to follow the cattle trail. That set of prints must have belonged to this Red Wind. Tofoya had become suspicious and set a trap. But where were the old warriors? They weren't on the rim of the canyon, gathering to rescue their friend. If they had been, Cody would have flushed them during the circle he had made.

Aware that nothing could be attempted till the Tofoyas and the men near the fire were asleep, Cody backtracked to the cliff. He found a narrow crevice, slipped into it, and sat down with his back to the hard, rough stone. Only one thing would bring him out before the men fell asleep—the beginning of the torture. If it did begin, Cody decided there was only one thing he could do. He would kill as many bandits as he could before they got him, which they would, of course, because of their numbers.

Cody sat and thought about Juan and Esteban

Tofoya. He recalled the atrocity stories that were widespread about their father, José. Apparently, the two boys, especially Juan, were chips off the old block. He thought also of the Indian, Red Wind. Where had he learned to speak such good English? Well, he would ask him, if they managed to get out of the canyon alive. One thing was for sure. He did not deserve the death that the comancheros had inflicted on Shorty Rhodes.

Finally, Cody allowed himself to doze, knowing that he wouldn't sleep long in a sitting position.

Cody came awake suddenly. He had a strong feeling that he had been awakened by something, and he sat very still and waited, his eyes searching the dark crevice. Had something come inside the fissure on him? He heard a dry slither that seemed to come from the floor, and then something began to pass over the toes of his boots. It paused a second, as if to consider what was beneath it, and then it moved on.

Cody froze, not daring to breathe, and listened to the sounds of rough scales or hide brush the leather of the boots. For what seemed like five minutes, he felt the slight pressure, and then it was gone. A moment later, in the better light beyond, he saw a six-foot rattlesnake continue to slither away. Then he became aware of the strong, musty scent that filled the crevice.

Rattlers denned together, Cody knew, and his first inclination was to scamper from the crevice as fast as he could. He checked that impulse, knowing that if there was another snake, the sudden movement would surely bring a strike. Then, very slowly, he pushed himself up, and with feet that felt like lead, he stepped into the open.

Standing in air free of the smell, he intended to take a deep breath, but for the moment he felt paralyzed, and the only thing he could manage was a spasm of trembling. When he had crawled into the crevice, he hadn't thought of snakes, an omission that might have proved fatal. Then, with a sinking feeling, Cody realized he had left the Winchester behind in the crevice.

He cursed himself silently, though he certainly understood the lapse. For a full minute he considered leaving the rifle where it was, but he knew it would be a foolhardy thing to do. With only a six-gun he would be at the mercy of the bandits in a fight. Gingerly, and with the care of a man walking on eggs, he eased back into the crevice. The musty snake scent now seemed stronger than ever, and Cody had the feeling he was surrounded by a bed of wriggling vipers where only minutes ago he had sat sleeping.

Reaching out a hand, he felt for the rifle he had leaned against the crevice wall. His hand touched the cold steel and he closed his fingers about the barrel. Then he backed out and stood in the cool night.

Cody wasn't known to be a religious man, but as he crossed to the boulder to peer into the comanchero camp again, he breathed a sigh of thanks to whatever had come to his aid in the crevice, for surely he had been lent a hand. Now if he could only hold on to that support for a little longer, he might get beyond the foolish thing he was about to attempt, foolish because of the danger he was about to subject himself to, and with no guarantee he would be able to rescue the Indian.

The fire had burned down to coals, and the camp was still and quiet except for a few snores. Cody could hear the low hum of bedded-down cattle from across the canyon. Overhead, the moon and stars seemed lower, and he could even make out the differently colored strata of the canyon wall. From up there somewhere a coyote wailed.

The bandits were stretched out about the fire. One lay no more than ten feet from the boulder Cody crouched behind. As Cody moved out to

circle the camp and come up on the Indian, he
had to pass within a step or so of the sleeping
comanchero. A coal snapped in the ashes, and
the man stirred. He made a turn in his blankets
and began to mumble. Cody was afraid he was
about to rouse up, and he dropped his hand to
the butt of the Colt, froze, and waited. But the
sleeper settled down.

A moment later he stood over the outstretched
Indian and looked down into his face. The man
was wide-awake, and Cody thought he saw a
flicker of something in his eyes, maybe recognition that Cody wasn't one of the bandits. Cody
put a finger to his lips. The Indian nodded.

Cody slashed with his bowie at the ropes that
bound the Indian's hands. Then he gave him the
rifle. Finally he cut free the man's feet and offered him a hand up. The Indian was shaky, but
he kept his balance.

"Let's get out of here," Cody whispered.

Instead, the Indian turned toward the sleeping men, slowly raised the rifle up, and took aim
at the nearest one. *The fool is about to commit
suicide for both of us,* Cody thought. Then he
drew the Colt.

"You pull that trigger and I won't wait for the
rest of that bunch to wake up and kill us," Cody
whispered hoarsely, ramming the six-gun into

the Indian's back. "I'll just save them half the effort."

The Indian stiffened, and they stood there for a long time before he lowered the rifle.

"Let's get out of here now," Cody whispered again.

They made the rocks, and stopped and looked back into the camp to make sure that the bandits still slept. No one had moved. "This way," Cody whispered, and headed toward the spot where he had left the mare.

"Do you have horses?" the Indian asked.

Again Cody marveled at the Indian's English. "I got just one, but she can carry double and get us out of here."

"Wouldn't take long to get another."

"No, I don't want that bunch stirred just yet. They're holding a woman and boy I've come for. I want them to lead me to wherever the captives are before they know I'm behind them."

"I know where they are being kept," the Indian said.

"Will you lead me there?"

"How could I refuse after what you did for me tonight? Their main camp is a day's ride west of here."

"Looks like we'll need another horse after all."

"Give me your knife and wait for me at the top of the slope that leads out of here."

"You sure you won't need some help?"

"Just wait for me up there," the Indian said with a sweep of his arm toward the exit from the deep canyon.

Cody gave him the knife, and the Indian faded into the darkness. Cody stood and took in the sounds of the canyon. There was still no stir in the camp, but the herd sounds would cover any noise that the comancheros' horses might make when the Indian approached them.

Reaching the spot where he had stashed the steeldust, Cody found that she had hardly moved though she had been left alone for hours. He gave her a quick couple of affectionate scratches about the base of the tuft of mane that fell over her face. Then he flicked the rein over her head and climbed into the saddle. As he sent the mare up the slope, the strain and creak of saddle leather sounded far too loud.

He topped out at the summit and pulled the mare up. Turning her about, he peered into the dark canyon and spotted the camp from a faint glow of what was left of the campfire. There was still no commotion there. He shifted his attention to the area of the canyon where the cattle were bedded, but distance and darkness kept them hidden.

As the wait stretched out, Cody began to feel that things hadn't gone well for the Indian in his quest for a horse. Then he caught the distinct sound of iron against rock at the base of the slope. A moment later a silhouette emerged from the shadows and climbed the slope.

"I was getting a little worried," Cody said as the Indian pulled up beside him.

"I took the time to pay off a little debt," the Indian replied. "One of the bandits guarding the cattle had punched me around earlier."

Cody looked over the mount the Indian had returned with, a long-legged dun gelding. "Looks like you came up with a good horse," he said.

"Good weapons too." He returned the Winchester and bowie to Cody.

"I hope you cleaned this," Cody said, examining the knife.

"Are you squeamish?" the Indian asked.

"Only about knives and guns. I hope you took something off that Mex you can use."

"He was well armed," the Indian replied. He patted the holstered six-gun around his waist. The butt of a rifle protruded from a saddle boot, and over his naked shoulders was a bandolier laced with cartridges.

"You did well, partner," Cody said. "Now point

out the direction we're to ride and we'll get out of here."

"West," the Indian said, and he took the lead.

Chapter Four

They were miles from the canyon when the sun came up. Cody had chewed only a little jerky over the last twenty-four hours, and he had a gnawing hunger. It was time also to give the horses a break. After checking their back-trail carefully for pursuit, he broached the possibility to Red Wind.

"There is a ravine ahead," the Indian said. "There should be water, and we can graze the horses."

"We'll chance a stop then," Cody replied.

He had pulled alongside Red Wind for the exchange, and for the first time he got a good look at his face. There were raw bruises on his cheeks. His lips were swollen, and the puffiness about his dark eyes had turned them into slits.

"They worked you over pretty good," Cody said.

"Yes. One had quite a technique with a boot."

Red Wind pointed to his side and grimaced slightly.

"Not as bad treatment as they gave the man they killed back at that ranch where they stole those cattle. They built a fire beneath his legs."

"Yes, one of them described that to me in vivid terms. He kept threatening me with that."

"Jesus Garcia?" Cody asked.

"How did you know?"

"I was behind a nearby boulder when the Tofoyas came back from their bath. I heard them call you Red Wind."

"My Indian name. What's yours?"

"Cody. Cody Carson."

"A combination of two very famous white men's names. At one time or another they were both known as friends to my people. Are they your kin?"

"Not Buffalo Bill Cody. I guess my ma just thought the two went well together. But I number old Kit among my ancestors. Hard for me to feature myself kin to a man like that."

"He would have been proud of what you did last night, Cody Carson . . . something I haven't thanked you properly for. I do that now."

"Accepted, but you'll more than repay that by leading me to Mary and Brad Tate." Cody had noted that the more serious Red Wind became, the more formal grew his English. It had become almost like from a book, and Cody became even more curious.

"She's a very beautiful woman," Red Wind said.

There was something thoughtful and pensive about the way Red Wind spoke, and for a moment Cody was struck by the quality it brought to the Indian's voice. He sounded a little like a man describing a loved one.

"You've seen her?" he asked.

"We keep an eye on the comancheros when they come out of Mexico. They know the location of our village. Over the years they've raided it many times. The village is always nervous when the comancheros prowl the llano. They are not now, nor were they ever, friends to my people."

"Mind if I put another question to you?" Cody asked.

"What would you like to know?"

"Where did you learn to jaw so well in English?"

"In school."

The brief, unexpected answer left Cody silent for a moment, but he couldn't leave it there. "In school, you say?" he asked.

Red Wind turned and looked at Cody. He gave what might have passed for a smile had his face been less stiff and sore. "You were expecting broken English?" he asked.

"Have to admit to something like that, I guess."

"And you're surprised at how I talk?"

"Well, you have to admit that your appearance and educated English don't usually go hand in hand."

"No, I guess they don't."

They rode in silence for a few minutes. Cody was reluctant to continue the questioning. Prolonged inquiries went against the grain with him, and Red Wind didn't seem to want to talk. Cody would have liked more information, but it would have to be volunteered.

"I was sent to the Indian school in Carlisle, Pennsylvania, when I was a boy," Red Wind said finally. "I stayed there until I was eighteen. Then I came back to the reservation."

There was bitterness in his voice. Apparently, his return to his people had not gone well. Cody knew something of reservation Indians. They were a whipped people and full of bitterness, especially the men. A young brave educated in the ways and language of the white man would have been a bitter pill for them to swallow.

"Your people didn't take to the new you," Cody said.

"I had become a white man to them. I represented everything the white man wanted to do to them. The old ways they loved so well had been educated out of me. They could see everything but the memories of the old wiped out in a single generation, and they turned their anger on the object they could see themselves coming to be."

He was silent, and Cody took a covert look. As Red Wind stared straight ahead, his naked torso seemed as stiff as a board beneath the Mexican bandolier. A muscle in his jaw began to twitch. His return to his people must have been an emotional plunge into a sea of acid. Cody tried to imagine what it must have been like. But he couldn't.

"I was to open a school," Red Wind continued, "and I did. My only students were a couple of girls. They were of mixed blood and fathered by whites. I think they thought that if they knew the language of their fathers, they might be able to leave the miserable life of the reservation. I did what I could for them. As for the young men, I had to fight them every day when I left the cabin that was supposed to be the school. I knew little of fighting, but I soon learned. It was either that or be beaten black-and-blue every afternoon."

"So you ran away to the Llano Estacado finally."

"Yes. I heard stories of Comanches who still lived the old life here, and I wanted to see what it was like. Of course, when I came, I didn't know if I would find anyone. I hadn't any proof that the stories weren't just that."

"But you did find someone."

"I had stolen a horse from the Army at Fort Sill. That horse and I crisscrossed this desert for weeks and I lived on lizards and snakes. The horse died first. I wouldn't have lasted much longer. I fell and lay there wondering if there was any use in trying to get up. Then I looked up and saw the faces of two old men as they leaned over me. They spoke to me in my native tongue. When I replied, they were more startled, I think, than when they first saw me. I was absolutely sure I was having a vision, for I had certainly fasted long enough, but they put me on a horse and took me back to the village. Man of Long Legs knew my father and mother. He took me in and helped to train me in the ways of my people."

Cody thought it a remarkable story, and he chewed on it during the silence that followed. There had seemed such pride in the little war party that had come upon him in the ravine. He recalled having compared the war party with Indians he had seen on reservations. These men were fighters and looked the part.

He had come along a little too late to get in on any Indian fighting in Texas, and he had always regretted that as he sat around and listened to the talk of older men. Now he wasn't so sure. He was beginning to like this Comanche.

He knew a little of the plight of defeated Indians, and he had sometimes felt sad about their lot, but never seriously. It wasn't something he was personally touched by. Had the question been put to him about what should have been done with the Indians, he would have replied that there seemed only two choices. Let them starve to death or teach them to live alongside the whites. Suddenly, he wasn't sure about those alternatives.

They came to the ravine and Red Wind led their descent into it. A shallow pan of water had collected in the lowest part of the ravine. A few cottonwoods and some Texas oaks surrounded the water, and there was some decent graze for the horses.

"You see to my hoss and I'll cook us up some breakfast," Cody offered.

"What about the smoke?" Red Wind asked.

"See them oaks? They're Texas oaks and those dry limbs will make less smoke than mesquite. I'll put our fire under one, and by the time the smoke filters up through those leaves, you won't be able to see it from the rim of the ravine. Of course, you could smell it. But this may be the last chance we have at something hot to eat for a spell. I think we'll risk it."

As Cody worked, he noted the care Red Wind gave the horses. And when they were well watered, he rubbed them down carefully with grass. Before staking them out to graze, he allowed each a wallow. Next he checked their legs for nicks and bruises. Cody was reminded of what he had always heard, that Comanches had a deep and abiding love for their horses.

With the smell of boiling coffee filling the ravine, Cody opened two cans of beans and dumped them into a frying pan. He sat the pan in the edge of the fire, not waiting for coals to collect. Then he opened a large can of peaches for dessert. The smell of the meal brought Red Wind to the fire. He eyed the peaches for a moment.

"I haven't had peaches since I left Pennsylvania," he said.

"Try a few while the beans get hot," Cody said, passing the can up to him.

Red Wind drew a long, wicked-looking knife from the belt of his loincloth with which to spear the peaches.

"Did you take that off the Mex too?" Cody asked.

"He couldn't have put it to use in his condition," Red Wind replied, spearing a peach.

They sat near the fire to eat, and there was no talk as they filled their bellies. When the edge was taken off his hunger, Cody said, "Tell me about your village. How many people are there?"

Red Wind studied Cody a moment before he spoke. He seemed to be trying to decide just how far this white man could be trusted.

"It's small," he said finally. "Some of the men who came here are dead. The rest are old. You saw four of them the other night. In the beginning the men numbered ten. Now there are only seven, counting me."

"And women and children?"

"The children number a dozen, but there are only four of the original women left. They have long since become too old to bear children. A few years ago Man of Long Legs led the warriors on a raid against a small Apache village and captured two women. They are still of childbearing age."

"Six women and seven men," Cody said. "Who's without a wife?"

"I have no woman," Red Wind said after a moment. "There is a girl in the village who will be old enough to marry in a few years. I believe it is the wish of Man of Long Legs that I should marry her."

Cody had the feeling that the secrets of the village had been bared to him, and he thought that Red Wind now seemed ill at ease. "You don't have to worry that I'll ever tell of your presence here," he said. "But there will come a time when the world will know. This desert will fill up with ranchers and sheepherders like the eastern llano. You'll have to contend with the white man once again."

"I know. Man of Long Legs speaks of that. We have come up with a plan."

Red Wind didn't volunteer what that plan was, nor did Cody ask. He figured that he'd been told enough, and from his appearance so did Red Wind.

"What about the Apaches? If you raided them for women, they would certainly return the visit."

"They do from time to time. There are Apaches south of us right now. I sent two of the warriors who were with me south to scout them. The other two returned to the village to help defend it in case of an attack by the comancheros or Apaches."

"And you stayed to scout the comancheros?"

"Yes."

"And got caught."

"They doubled back and set a trap for me. Like a fool, I rode into it."

They began to clean their cooking utensils, and for a while there was silence between them, the comfortable silence of two men who had begun to relax with each other.

Then Red Wind said, "You know my history, but I've heard nothing of yours." Something in his voice suggested to Cody that the Comanche would be offended if the balance wasn't corrected. Like most Texans, Cody was reluctant to speak of himself, but he felt he owed Red Wind something, since the Indian had spoken so freely of himself, mostly at Cody's prodding.

"My pa was killed trying to bring peace between two feuding families in east Texas. He was shot down in broad daylight when it was rumored he had taken sides with one faction against the other. He lived long enough to make me swear not to get drawn into the killing. I told him I couldn't stand by and watch his killers go unpunished. He said, 'Get yourself a badge then and do it legal.'"

"I know you got yourself the badge," Red Wind said, "but did you get your father's killers?"

"No, but other Rangers did, which, as it turned out, was best for all."

They packed the utensils away after rinsing

them in the shallow pool. "Woman's work," Red Wind commented wryly.

"But a man who ain't got no woman has to do it himself," Cody said, smiling. "You bring in the horses while I bury these hot ashes."

A few minutes later they rode out of the ravine and headed west again. Cody hadn't told Red Wind all that much about himself, but the Indian seemed satisfied.

"That is the camp," Red Wind said, indicating the vista spread out beneath.

Cody and Red Wind lay behind a line of rock that was the spine of a low ridge to the east of the comanchero camp. They had left their mounts well down the east side of the ridge and made their way carefully up to the point where they could view what was happening below.

The size of the camp surprised Cody. Four crude buildings had been hastily erected to the south of another low ridge covered with mesquite and brush. The buildings were constructed of cottonwood logs taken from trees bordering the ridge to the north. They seemed only semi-permanent affairs, for their roofs were nothing more than leafy branches held in place by heavier limbs crisscrossing to hold the other limbs in place. Though they were some distance away, Cody could smell the curing leaves and

Last Warriors on the Llano 75

lumber. The log frames did suggest one thing, however. The Tofoyas planned to increase their intrusions into the llano.

About the buildings stood six of the lumbering, two-wheeled carts in which comancheros had for a century or more crossed the desert as they quested for trade with the Comanches. As high as a man's head, the wheels were of wood, and only recently had the custom of rimming the wheels with a band of iron been adopted. The cumbersome vehicles were usually pulled by yokes of oxen.

To the south of the camp grazed a herd of horses. The thin grass was no doubt nourished by the underground water that kept the cottonwoods growing. That grass, more than the water, very likely was the chief reason that the Tofoyas had chosen the site. Cody estimated the horses to number a hundred or more, which suggested that ranches other than Beaver Creek had been hit. The herd, not to mention the cattle being driven in, represented a lot of loot with which the Tofoyas would return to Mexico.

"Juan Tofoya's got a small army down there," Cody said to Red Wind.

"Mexican labor is cheap," Red Wind replied. "A little bread, a peso or two, and he can hire all the men he needs, especially if it represents a chance to steal from the gringos. The Hispanos hate the white eyes almost as much as the red man does." A slight smile on Red Wind's face took much of the sting out of the comment for Cody.

"You seem to be informed on the subject of the Mexicans," Cody said. "How come?"

"I have crossed the border a few times in the last two years. I've picked up information on such trips."

"You didn't go dressed as you are now, I'll bet," Cody joked, taking in the loincloth that was still the Indian's only dress. "Mexicans have no love for Comanches, and they would have spotted you for one at once. You wouldn't have lasted the length of two breaths before they strung you up. They would have thought you had come for their women and horses, as Comanches have done for centuries."

Red Wind smiled at the joke, and he was silent for a moment as he considered what Cody had said. "The old men still talk of those times," he replied. "When they sit about the village fire and recite the history of the Comanches for the children, those raids are always part of the story. They still plan those raids when the season approaches, but even they know that six old men would not last long down there. No, I do not go as a warrior. I slip into peasant clothes. I speak a little Spanish and pass for a mestizo. That's one way I have learned to use what the white eyes taught me in that school."

Again the sting in the Indian's words was softened by his smile, and Cody took no offense at the remark. In fact, he rather enjoyed hearing Red Wind bring the longtime enmity between whites and Indians into the open in such a healthy way. Joking references often blunted the rabid edges of such relationships. And he was joking about his own fate as well. A man who could do that, even if the jokes were slight ones, was a man who had come to terms with what he was.

That thought revealed something else to Cody. Though he had spent only a brief time with this educated Indian, he had come to like and respect him despite the garb and the war paint.

"If we're going to get the Tates out of there, we have to do it tonight," he said. "The Tofoyas are less than a day behind us, and they'll come riding in here no later than tomorrow morning. That would make our job a lot harder."

"At least, we might have a chance at the Tofoyas then," Red Wind said.

"I wouldn't mind that, partner," Cody replied, "but my chief concern for now is to get the Tates out of there. After that, we might plan something for the Tofoyas. Besides, the Tofoyas might give the order to pull up stakes and head for Mexico, which could sure make this job harder."

"Yes, but the moon will be full. If they know the Apaches are prowling the llano, they will double the guard. Getting in and out of the camp won't be easy."

"Don't that many horses just make a Comanche warrior's mouth water?" Cody said, leading up to the plan forming in his mind. "I'm hoping your attention don't get diverted from what we came here for. Of course, you might get a little fun out of sending that herd off in all directions sometime late tonight. With the comancheros thinking the Apaches have struck, they'll be apt to leave that camp as empty as an old jaybird's nest. I hope you can remember you're just stampeding them, though, and don't decide to filch a few. I know that horseflesh like that is apt to get a Comanche brave excited."

Though Cody kept his face straight and his voice dry, Red Wind turned and gave him a long stare. "Indians may have invented and perfected the art of horse stealing," he said, "but the whites took to it like foxes raiding a den of prairie dogs. Some of the wrinkles they came up with would make Comanche horse thieves look like amateurs."

Cody couldn't hold back his laughter and he

had to smother his face against the rock to keep the sound from carrying down the hillside. "You got me there, partner," he said. "I spend a lot of my time trying to unravel those tricks."

Red Wind did not join in the laughter, but there was an unmistakable look of friendship in his eyes as he stared into Cody's face. The look suggested he had begun to change a few opinions of his own.

"Which building are the captives kept in?" Cody asked after a moment.

"The one to the west."

"Both the boy and the girl?"

"Twice I have seen them come from that building early in the morning."

That suggested to Cody that Red Wind had spent a lot of time watching the comanchero camp, perhaps more than was needed just to scout their intentions. Cody recalled the way Red Wind had sounded when he spoke of Mary Tate earlier.

"How close in were you?" he asked.

"I watched from the ridge at the back of the buildings."

"Well, will you look at that!" Cody whispered, indicating the building Red Wind had just pointed out.

A woman had just stepped from the building. She wore denim pants tucked into three-quarter boots. A blue work shirt completed her apparel, but Cody's eyes lingered longest on the blond hair that fell almost to her shoulders. She was a tall woman, and there was a strength in the way she stood.

She turned slowly, her eyes searching the distance in each direction. Clearly, she was looking for something. For the dreaded return of the Tofoyas? Or did she possess the hope that someone would ride to her rescue? Possibly Goodnight and some of his riders? When Mary Tate's eyes reached the spot on the ridge where Cody and Red Wind lay, she seemed to keep them there for a moment, as though she had discovered their presence on the ridge. She was a woman, Cody knew, who was used to studying cliffs and rises, and she had no doubt studied this ridge a few times since her capture. Had she noticed something different in the contour of the ridge where they lay? Then her gaze moved on. A moment later she turned and entered the building.

Cody heard a low sigh as Red Wind released his breath. Turning his head, he studied the Indian's face. Red Wind's eyes were glued to the door through which Mary Tate had disappeared. *He's in love with her*, Cody thought, and he wondered if those feelings would complicate things if they succeeded in getting her from the camp.

But why he would think so, he had no idea. Red Wind was too civilized to try to force himself on a woman.

"Can you figure out a way to get those horses running?" Cody asked.

"There will be a moon tonight, but I'll manage."

"They'll probably double the guard, so be careful."

"They won't spot me."

"You won't be nervous?"

"Why should I be?"

"Well, I always heard that Indians didn't take to exposing themselves too much at night. Something about their spirits not finding their way back to wherever spirits want to go."

"Did you never hear of a Comanche moon?" Red Wind asked.

"It's supposed to be the only time Comanches raid at night."

"Well, that's what we'll have tonight."

There was a slight edge to Red Wind's voice, and as he stared silently at the comanchero camp, Cody wondered if his unease had to do with Mary Tate or something that he, Cody, had said.

"What is it, partner?" he asked. "You seem a bit out of joint."

"Nothing."

"Must be something . . . the way you're scowling."

"Maybe we can talk about it later," Red Wind replied. "Right now we should get off this ridge. It's far too exposed to the east, and I've been watching that dust tailing up back there."

Cody turned for a look. There was, indeed, dust. "That's a good half day back," he said.

"The Tofoyas might send riders ahead. They might even come themselves. They would have to be a little anxious about the fortune they've got waiting for them here."

"Including what they intend to get for Mary Tate," Cody added.

"You heard them talking, then?"

"Yes."

They lay on the ridge for a while. Red Wind watched the house as Cody studied the ridge behind it, for that was the way he would have to approach the camp when he came into it later that night.

"Wonder what they intend to do with the boy?" he asked suddenly. "They might just keep him around to keep his sister better pacified till they sell her. But what then? Kill him?"

"I doubt it," Red Wind said. "There are markets for boys as well. A white boy might bring a fancy price in some circles."

"Lord help us to keep both of them from such a fate," Cody said.

"Amen," Red Wind replied, and the word sounded strange indeed when uttered by an Indian in a loincloth.

Chapter Five

Cody glanced at the night sky, and he decided he had never seen a night so bright. The moon had still to rise, and when it did, the llano would be lit as brightly as day, which certainly would make the job of slipping into the comanchero camp a lot more difficult. Red Wind's job of stampeding the horse herd would be made more dangerous too.

The two were now on the ridge overlooking the four buildings. Just beneath them was the building in which Mary and Brad Tate were being held. They had taken refuge beneath a willow that managed somehow to suck enough water for survival from the slope, a sign that the water that seeped from beneath the base of the slope and watered the meadows to the south was very near the surface. The whiplike branches of the tree hung almost to the ground to form a huge umbrella beneath which the two men lay. There were a few signs, if one looked closely, of previous occupation, and Cody knew without asking that Red Wind had lain beneath the willow to watch Mary Tate when she came from her prison building.

Cody's stomach rumbled emptily. Red Wind looked at him and smiled. There had been no time since the early morning meal to cook and eat . . . just the jerky to chew. A man's stomach could only take so much jerky, even washed down with water. There had been no sleep, either, and Cody felt his eyelids grow heavy as they sat in the deep shade.

The night so resembled the day that Cody could see the confused fly that suddenly buzzed about his head. A small night bird drifted into the top limbs of the willow, and for a moment its song floated eerily along the ridge. Then, becoming aware of the intruders beneath, it flew away hastily. Cody could feel Red Wind's apprehension at the sudden flight of the bird. It was the sort of sound and movement to warn suspicious eyes and ears below. To their rear the grass rustled as some rodent moved through in search of food.

Their plans for the rescue of the Tates were long since complete, and they were simple enough. Red Wind would circle the camp and stampede the horses. The bandits would probably assume an Apache attack, and the camp would empty south to save the herd. Having positioned himself near the building in which the Tates were held, Cody would then bring out the captives and would retreat with them up the hill where they would wait for Red Wind's return. If all went well, they would then ride north to Red Wind's village.

The ride to the village was Red Wind's idea. He had insisted on it, saying that the bandits would never suspect an escape to the north, and since, even in the bright light of this night, they wouldn't be able to track very well, they would assume that the escape route was to the east, and surge in that direction. By the time they realized their mistake, Cody and Red Wind with the Tates would have several hours head start. Cody could find no fault with the plan. Still, something buzzed a warning in his head.

There was only one problem—mounts for the Tates. But there was a possibility. Behind one of the buildings was a small corral with a dozen or so horses. Apparently held ready for emergencies, they were kept saddled and ready. They were changed daily, and just before sundown, Cody and Red Wind had watched fresh horses brought in and saddled up while the horses in the corral were led out.

The saddled mounts were tempting, but, according to Red Wind, they were always under guard. The guard would have to be taken out, and there lay the danger. A hundred things could go wrong and alert the whole camp.

"You will have to make a decision when you get down there," Red Wind had advised. "If you see a chance, take it. If not, we will make our escape doubled up."

And so the matter had rested. As the time approached to make their move, Cody's mind went back to the plan to ride north to the village. His thoughts dwelled on Red Wind's insistence that they adopt the plan. Was it the Indian's insistence that was troubling? And had that insistence something to do with Red Wind's obvious preoccupation with Mary Tate? Such a suspicion was unfounded, Cody decided. Thus far, Red Wind had done nothing to justify such thoughts.

Besides, Cody was curious. Since hearing Red Wind's story, he had developed an interest in the village. He wanted to see the small group of Comanches who had found a place deep in the desert where they could continue their traditional way of life, where the encroaching ways of whites had not touched them yet. And Cody kept remembering the comment that Red Wind had made about the chief, Man of Long Legs, and Red Wind's having come up with a way to preserve their sanctuary in the llano. He found himself wondering what that solution was.

"It is time, my friend," Red Wind said, and pushed himself up.

Cody stood up and they faced each other. Reaching a hand out, he took Red Wind's hand in his. "I owe you, *amigo*," he said. "But not so much as Mary Tate and the boy will owe you."

"You more than paid me for anything I'll do," Red Wind reminded him.

"I'd like you to know I look on you as a friend," Cody said. He still held the Indian's hand, and now he gave it a warm grip.

"And I you ... whatever happens."

Then Red Wind was gone, and Cody was left to ponder the meaning of the cryptic remark. He wondered if Red Wind was troubled by some premonition of disaster. He put the thought from his mind then and began a slow, careful descent of the slope.

When he reached the last of the trees that bordered the rear of the building, he stopped and sought to locate the guard on the corral. The boulder on which the man had sat earlier was now empty, and Cody decided that the fates had favored him after all. Then, beyond the corral there was movement, and he saw the man. To keep himself awake, he had begun to pace back and forth. The man turned and came back toward Cody. Would he take his position on the rock or continue? Pausing before the corral, the man seemed to consider the rock. Then he moved in Cody's direction.

Pressing himself against the bole of the tree, Cody waited. He hardly dared to hope the man would come so far. If he did, and if Cody could silence him, the extra horses would speed their escape.

As the man came on, Cody slipped the bowie from its sheath, making sure the blade did not flash a warning in the bright night. The man began to hum a lively Mexican tune.

Then the man was there, and Cody reached out an arm to encircle his head and clamp a hand over his mouth. Simultaneously, he put the edge of the bowie's blade against the exposed throat and pulled. By the time Cody dragged him into the shadow of the tree, the man's death struggles had ceased. After cleaning the bowie on the man's clothes, Cody sheathed it, walked to the corral, selected the two best horses, and finally eased the others from the corral and turned them loose. When Red Wind spooked the herd, Cody suspected that the loose horses would hear and join in the run. He led the two horses back into the trees on the slope, then returned to the back of the building that housed the Tates.

The moon hung to the east and cast a slim

shadow along the west side of the building. Keeping to that, Cody made the front corner and peered around and saw the burly form of a guard before the door. He stood there and tried to decide what there was he could do. Sheer luck had brought the corral guard to him, but there was no indication that this one had any thought of moving. If he was to have a chance at him, Cody would have to make the approach.

As if to stress the unlikelihood of any movement from him, the guard struck a match and lit a cigarette. Cody had to move quickly to avoid the glare of the match. At that moment, the first of the gunshots to the south exploded.

The man's first reaction was a grunt of surprise. For another second he seemed frozen in his position before the door. Then he stepped out from the building to peer to the south. His back was to Cody now, and there was the chance to make a move. From the south came more shots, and faint shouts of alarm from the guards. The noise drew the guard farther from the building.

Then men poured out of the next building. Some were only half dressed. They swarmed between the buildings toward the corral. Another moment and the night was filled with their frustrated curses.

That commotion was more than the guard on the building could withstand. First he stepped to the corner of the building and peered around at the corral. Then he disappeared. It was the opportunity Cody was waiting for, and he raced along the front of the building, gave the door a push, and stepped in.

"Who is it?" a woman cried out. "What do you want? Get out of here!"

"My name is Carson and I'm a Texas Ranger. I've come for you and the boy."

There was total silence.

"Ma'am?"

"Yes."

"Did you hear me?"

"I did."

"Where's the boy? We've got to get out of here. We have only seconds before that guard returns."

"I'm here," a boy said.

"We're coming," Mary Tate said.

Still, there was no movement except for a rustling sound, as if someone was bundling something.

"Don't pack anything, ma'am. Just come as you are," Cody ordered urgently.

"I don't think you want me to do that, Mr. Carson," came the reply. "I had slipped out of my britches and I'm putting them back on."

"In that case we can spare a second or two, I reckon. I hope the boy is dressed, though."

"I am."

Cody heard the move across the room then, and they brushed up against him. There was the clean scent of the woman, and his hand brushed the top of the boy's head. With the pair behind him, Cody eased the door open and looked for the guard. He was nowhere to be seen.

"Come on," he whispered, and herded Mary and Brad Tate before him.

As they raced for the corner of the building and its cover, the sound of running horses could be heard to the south. The men who had swarmed to the corral were now headed south on foot. There was the sound of more gunfire, and it seemed to be following the running herd of horses. Cody hoped that none of it was aimed at Red Wind.

They were within a few steps of the corner of the building when Cody glanced to his rear and saw the guard. The man was bringing his rifle up to shoot. "Move!" Cody shouted, but he knew it was too late. The rifle boomed and a ton of bricks struck Cody about midway down his back. He was thrown forward and knocked flat on his face.

He didn't pass out, however. Gathering what strength he could muster, he rolled to his back in time to see the guard above him brandishing the rifle as a club. Cody reached for the Colt and managed to draw it before the rifle descended. The six-gun exploded, as did the dark face just above him.

Cody felt hands lifting him, and a second later he was upright, Mary on one side, the boy on the other. Together they steered him along the building.

"Up the ridge!" Cody cried. "I've got horses there!"

They ran as fast as they could across the moonlit stretch between the house and the trees, but the pace was frustratingly slow.

"Maybe you should leave me," Cody muttered. "Take the horses. I have a friend who'll meet you at the summit of the ridge. He'll be dressed like a savage, but don't be afraid of him."

"Don't be ridiculous!" Mary Tate snapped. "We can't desert you after you risked your life to rescue us! Just save your breath and work your legs instead of your mouth!"

Cody admired her spunk, but he wasn't so sure of her wisdom. He could feel the warm blood drenching his back, and he knew he was getting weaker. At the same time, the trees that had seemed so near seemed to be moving. He stumbled, and Mary put an arm about his waist to help keep him upright. Cody's almost delirious thought was that the arm was going to have an awful lot of blood on it when it was withdrawn.

"There!" Cody said as they approached the two horses he had taken from the corral. "The other is beneath the willow a bit farther up."

"I know that tree," Mary said. "I've seen it when they let me out for a walk. You just hold on and we'll get you on one of these."

"Ain't got the time for that," Cody muttered. "Just gimme a hold on the saddle horn! Then get these hosses up the slope!"

"All right," Mary agreed, but she sounded doubtful that Cody could hold on to anything, much less a horse moving up a slope.

He managed it, however, using all his strength just to hang on, and letting the horse pull his dragging feet. But he paid a price. As the horse pulled him along, demons were on his back, and they seemed to be working on him with knives.

The steeldust gave a whinny of recognition as well as alarm as they reached the willow. "Easy, girl," Cody told her, and then he said to Mary, "Ain't nobody else can ride this hoss without a good bucking, which we ain't got time for. You'll have to help me up on her."

He staggered to the mare and pulled himself up while Mary and Brad pushed and hoisted. Finally, he managed to swing his leg over the mare and settled into the saddle. "Up there." He pointed. "We're to meet my friend up there. Remember what I said about how he'll look."

"Why do you keep warning us, Mr. Carson?" Mary asked. "Are you traveling with some kind of monster?"

"You'll see," was the only explanation Cody felt like making.

Brad took the lead while Mary rode alongside Cody to keep him in the saddle. Cody managed to get his first real look at her.

The moonlight fell across her face, and he knew he had seldom seen such beauty in a woman. The blond hair, in some disarray, fell about her face, but it didn't hide the classical features, and though her eyes were in shadow, Cody knew they would be blue. No wonder Red Wind had taken such a fancy to her. What man wouldn't?

Surprisingly, Red Wind was already on the ridge and waiting.

"Miss Tate...Brad, meet my friend, Red Wind."

Then Cody wasn't sure he was Red Wind at all, for somewhere...somehow...the Indian had changed his garb. He no longer wore the loincloth. Instead, he had donned a surprisingly fresh and clean suit of peasant clothes.

"Where in heaven did you..." Cody began.

Then the world began to swirl about him. He

reached out to grab hold of something in an effort to keep himself upright, but his hands found only air. Still, he did not fall, and he thought he felt Mary's gentle arms about him once more, and then stronger arms. He couldn't be sure, however, for he was rapidly falling into a swirling well of darkness.

Chapter Six

The light seemed a long way off before it began to drift closer. Then Cody became aware of the swaying motion, as if he were suspended in a very tight swing. The swinging was accompanied by a scraping sound that seemed very familiar. Finally, he opened his eyes.

He saw Mary first. She was about ten feet back and she rode a big roan-colored horse that was decked out in a big Mexican saddle. She was dragging a tree limb behind the horse to wipe out their trail. A steady stream of dust rolled up behind the limb. For a moment Cody was puzzled by the presence of the woman and by her attempting to wipe out their trail. Then his memory hooked in and he recalled in a flash the series of events leading up to his taking the bullet.

He pushed himself up for a look around and paid the price as spurts of pain shot along his back, zigzagging wildly. He rode out the pain, though, and was rewarded by solving the mystery of the swaying motion as well as the scraping sound. He was being hauled along in a travois formed by lacing his blanket onto two poles crossed at their small ends and harnessed to the steeldust with ropes. The boy rode ahead and led the mare. As Mary shouted something, the travois stopped.

Pulling her mount up beside Cody, she stepped down. Recalling her beauty in the moonlight, he decided that the night had not done her justice. He was sure he had never seen a more beautiful woman. She placed a cool hand on his forehead, and Cody had the strong impression he had felt those hands before, and for the first time in a very long time he couldn't think of a word to say, not even hello.

"Well, you still don't have any fever, which is good," Mary said. "But how do you feel?"

"Like I just fought a grizzly bear and got whipped. I know I was shot, but how bad is it?"

"Not as bad as it might have been. You lost a lot of blood before we could stop and get the bullet out. That's the worst part. The wound will be sore, but it'll heal over in a couple of days if there's no infection. I don't think there will be, since there's no fever."

She had moved her hand and stood above him,

and Cody realized he had some memory of Mary as well as Red Wind working over him. The sunlight danced off her blond hair, and something deep inside Cody responded to the dazzling picture, something very deep and powerful. Its current seemed to sap the rest of his strength. He became aware then that their eyes were still locked in a gaze. Her eyes were brown rather than blue, and he decided that brown was an improvement. Color suddenly crept up her neck and into her face, and he noted the slight bridge of freckles that spread across her nose and upper cheeks.

"I went through your saddlebags and found your gauze and bandages," she said. "I hope you don't mind."

"I'm obliged to you."

The silence between them seemed to crackle. Cody found his tongue first. "Maybe you could tell me where Red Wind is," he said. "I don't see him around anywhere."

"He went back to scout the bandits. They're already after us, you know."

"What time of day is it, and how long has Red Wind been gone?"

"It's afternoon, and he's been gone since the middle of the morning. His instructions were for us to keep traveling north. We should pick up a hogback soon. It runs north and south, and we're to follow that till he catches up with us. He said he'd try to find us before nightfall."

"Are you sure they're behind us?" Cody asked, wondering how the Tofoyas had gotten on the trail so soon, because they wouldn't have reached the camp until morning.

Mary turned and pointed to their rear. "Unless that's a dust storm back there, they're after us. I don't think it is a storm, since it's been there since daybreak and gaining all the while."

Even on the travois Cody could see the dust, and for a full minute he considered their predicament. He was flat on his back—well, not quite, since that was where the wound was—and he was responsible for a woman and a boy who had already been the captives for several days of the varmints in pursuit. Cody had overheard most of their plans for the woman, and he had no intention of letting her fall into their hands again. Some of his resolve, he knew, was based on the way he had begun to feel about her, though he was not ready to put a name to those feelings. Easing his legs over the side of the travois, he sat up.

"What are you doing?" Mary said. She lay a hand on his shoulder as if to restrain him.

"I'm about to stand up." Cody gritted his teeth against the crisscrossing pain in his back.

"You'll start to bleed all over again."

"Maybe, but if we don't get a move on, we'll all face worse than that." Cody recalled the mutilation of Shorty Rhodes and the threats to Red Wind he had overheard, and he decided on the spot that if he was to die at the hands of the Tofoyas, he would choose his own manner of dying. He would go down with a gun in his hand, and if he had the strength to hold it up and pull the trigger, he would take Tofoya or some of his men with him.

He pushed himself up from the travois and stood on his feet. For a moment the landscape circled and tilted about him. Then he found his balance. Reaching for his knife, he found the sheath empty. "Where's the bowie?" he asked Mary.

She turned and walked back to the roan. Her stride suggested what she thought of a man who wouldn't listen to good advice. She returned with the knife in her hand.

"I used it to probe for the bullet in your back."

He took it but didn't move away at once. "I really do thank you for everything you did. I really do. It's just that I'm like an old bull out in the wild. I've lived alone on the trail so much that I've lost the knack for manners and such. I hope you'll take that into account if I rub you the wrong way... which I sure will if the past is any indication of my conduct with folks."

The words might not have been formal, but their delivery certainly was . . . almost courtly in a rural sort of way. That surprised Cody mightily, and he could see some effect in the round brown eyes before him.

"What did you intend to do with the knife?" she asked quietly.

"Cut my blanket from those poles."

"Let me do it for you."

She took the knife from his hand and, bending over the travois, began to slice the cords. Cody moved to the front and began to work at the rope harness with fingers weaker than he could recall ever having before.

They finished at about the same time.

"You'll be wanting your Colt too," she said. "I've been carrying it on the horn of my saddle, just in case."

She returned to the roan while Cody stuffed the blanket back into his bedroll.

"She ain't used to people not taking her advice," a voice said.

Turning, Cody saw the boy. He was still up, and he looked particularly small in the big, cumbersome Mexican saddle upon a rawboned red mare. He was a cottontop who looked very much like his sister, and he did have blue eyes.

"You must be Brad," Cody said.

"Yes, sir. My sister don't like it when folks

don't do as she tells them. She seems to be taking it better from you than she did with Pa, Shorty, and me back at the ranch."

"You talk too much, Brad," Mary said, returning with the holstered Colt. She extended it to Cody.

The boy responded with a slight smile and a quick wink at Cody. Buckling the holster about his hips, Cody decided that he liked the boy. He turned and studied the tail of dust that boiled up behind them, and was shocked at how much closer it now was. "We'd best be getting under way," he said, stepping to the steeldust.

He reached a hand up to the saddle horn and then brought his foot up to the stirrup, a maneuver he could barely accomplish. Then he felt hands grab his belt from behind to give him a hoist, and he managed to swing his other leg up and over and settle into the saddle. When he looked down, he was staring into Mary's face.

"You thanked me earlier for what I did for you," she said. "That wasn't much, considering the risks you've put yourself to for our sake. I just want you to know we appreciate that. Don't we, Brad?"

"Yes, sir, we do, Mr. Carson."

The title sounded so strange, even coming from the boy, that Cody had to protest it. "I'd be proud if both of you called me Cody," he said.

"Cody it'll be then," Mary said. "But with one condition."

"What's that?"

"While you were under and a few other times, you've called me 'ma'am.' My name is Mary."

Cody felt his face go hot. There were all those vague memories in his mind of her working over him, of those cool hands. If his tongue had come loose and he had talked . . . ! What else had he said?

"I hope I didn't say much that was foolish when I was doing that talking," he managed.

The smile she gave him wasn't all that reassuring, and he felt the heat attack his face again. Mary's response was to turn, walk back to the roan, and climb into the saddle.

"Your Indian friend told me to drag this limb over the ground," Mary said. "Shall I continue?"

"Drop it," Cody replied. "What we have to do is put distance between us and that dust. We can't take time right now to hide our sign."

They got under way then, riding three abreast, with Cody in the middle. Glancing to the west, he measured the sun. Not more than two or three hours of daylight left, he decided. They could use that time to keep the Tofoyas from gaining. When darkness fell, they would gain some advantage, because the comancheros would have to slow down to do their tracking.

When that happened, Cody was determined to put a lot of distance between the Tofoyas and this party of three.

Cody couldn't help but wonder where Red Wind was. The village was to the north, and presumably they might find it even without Red Wind, but what would the old chief and the ancient warriors do if they came riding in without the young warrior, especially when they learned the Tofoyas were hot on their trail?

But that wasn't the extent of his concern. Cody had come to respect the Indian and even consider him a friend. He hoped Red Wind didn't fall into the hands of the Tofoyas again. Jesus Garcia, the one who loved to apply the torture so much, would surely dream up something special for the red man who had escaped him once before. Just as he would cook up something for the Ranger who had helped in that escape. That thought made Cody turn to study the dust again.

Cody caught his first glimpse of the hogback, a bluish slab of granite that rose out of the desert landscape like the scaly back of a lizard and then became a full-fledged ridge.

"That's it," Mary said. "It's just as Red Wind described it."

They rode in silence toward the hogback for a while. Cody was very aware of the riders on either side. He felt almost as ill at ease with the boy as he did with Mary. Kids, even boys, were strangers to him. Still, he couldn't help but be impressed by Brad. The boy had undergone many days of captivity by as fearsome a bunch as the imagination could dream up, and he seemed to have come out of it as well as anyone could.

"I haven't asked you about home," Mary said.

She rode on Cody's left, and as she spoke, she turned to stare toward the lowering sun. She made a lovely silhouette against the gradually coloring western sky, Cody decided.

"Your father was killed in that first raid," Cody said sadly. "Did you know that?"

"Not for sure, but we suspected it from what we overheard." Mary spoke as though she had reconciled herself to her father's death. Then she said, "We knew when they went back for the cattle. We were hoping Shorty wouldn't be there. Was he?"

"I'm afraid he was."

"He's dead too, then?"

"Yes."

"He was like one of the family. He and Pa served in the cavalry together. He was a corporal and in charge of the company's horses. When they left the Army, they took up the land in Beaver Creek Canyon together. I suppose it belongs to Brad and me now, though I'm not sure I ever want to see the place again."

"They burned the house down," Cody said. "Where will the two of you live when we get back?"

She turned and studied the dust. "*If* we get back."

"I promise you we will ... somehow."

"I almost believe you."

She gave him a smile, and Cody felt one of the knots that formed in his heart each time he looked at her. She was even more beautiful when the sun struck her face as it did then.

"Why did your pa and Shorty settle there in the first place?" he asked. "Seems like a lonely place to bring up a family. No schools, no neighbors. Must have been a lonesome kind of life though it's beautiful country."

"Yes, it is," she said, and was silent again. Cody wasn't sure she would respond to his question, and he was content to let it drop. Then she said, "They were with Colonel McKenzie when he surprised the Comanches there. They saw the place and they liked it. It was about the time ranchers in the Panhandle began to put up barb fences. I guess they thought they'd save on fence."

"Did you ever visit Bone Canyon?" he asked.

"A few times. It always depressed me. Pa and

Shorty helped with the killing of the horses, or had you heard?"

It was information that Cody wished she hadn't given him, but the sadness with which she spoke the words suggested it was something she needed to share with him, or with someone, at least. The thought occurred to him that meeting Red Wind might have had something to do with bringing the slaughter of the horses to her mind.

"Pa and Shorty had decided to sell out to Mr. Goodnight," she said. "I suppose Mr. Goodnight will still want to buy it."

"Where will you and Brad live?" Cody asked again. The answer was important to him.

"Pa was planning to buy a half interest in a hardware store in El Paso. I don't suppose there will now be much to attract us there."

"Why not?" Cody asked. "It's a nice place to live. Mostly Mexicans, of course, but with the exception of the likes back there, I always liked them."

"I feel the same way, but what would there be for me to do?"

"Teach school?"

"I haven't enough education to do that. That leaves sewing and waiting on tables. I'd just as soon work in a hardware store as do either." As she paused she seemed to consider what she had just said. "Did you ever stop and think how few choices a woman has for work if she decides not to marry?" she asked, her voice bitter suddenly.

"No, I can't say I ever thought too much about that," Cody said. "I just never thought too much about marriage at all."

She gave him a look that seemed to wither something inside him. He fumbled for something to say, but could only come up with a couple of grunts, and even they did not come out easily.

"Most men don't," she said. "Till the bug hits them. Then they prance around and ply a woman with their favors. When the woman gives in, the man is loving and protective for a few months, but then he turns her into a beast of burden like all his other animals." The bitterness in her words was scorching. Cody had never heard a woman speak in such a manner. He thought of Red Wind and his attraction to her. How would even an educated Indian turn a woman like Mary into the traditional Comanche squaw? The thought brought a smile to Cody's face. Unfortunately, Mary saw it.

"You find all that amusing, do you?" she asked. Anger flooded her face, turning the brown eyes as dark as a storm.

"No. I—"

"Never mind!" she snapped, and kneed the

roan until she rode well ahead of Cody and her brother.

"She keeps remembering the way Ma died," Brad said.

"How *did* she die?" Cody asked.

"I don't rightly remember. I was too small, but Mary says she worked herself to death cooking and doing chores. In the spring she even helped out on the range. Mary vows that'll never happen to her."

"Then why did she stay on in Beaver Creek Canyon?"

"When Ma died, she made Mary promise to stay and look after me. She told me about that not too long ago. I said I was big enough to look after myself now, and if that was what was holding her back, she could go. I even offered to go with her."

"What did she say?"

"She asked me how she would make a living for us . . . work in a saloon?" Cody felt the boy's eyes on him, as if probing for something. "I had to ask Shorty what kind of work that was. When I found out, I decided I didn't want her to do it. Do you blame me?"

The speech sounded so innocent that Cody almost smiled again. Remembering the outburst after his previous smile, he kept his face straight. "No," he said, "you're not to be blamed for that. It's not the work for her. On top of that, your sister might just decide to change the rules of one of those establishments."

"She can sure be as tough and determined as an old mule," the boy agreed thoughtfully.

They had passed the lizard's tail of the hog-back by then, and the taller part of the ridge was looming up rapidly. Low brush grew along its base, and Cody studied the growth for some sign of cottonwood, the surest sign that they might find water in the brush. The growth was mostly mesquite, which was too bad, because the horses needed a drink. And Cody's canteen had almost been emptied after the last time he passed it around.

Then he recalled something an old mustanger had once told him: "Son, if you're ever in the desert and find yourself getting thirsty, remember that wild horses eat mesquite seed. You'd be surprised how often they dump them seed out right after they've watered up. Then them seeds come up. Information like that can come in handy, son."

Cody began to search out the tallest and the greenest of the trees. When he spotted what he was looking for, he pulled up and studied the dust behind them for about the hundredth time. He found some consolation in the fact that for the last two hours they seemed to be holding their own against the pursuit. If anything, the dust was dropping back or maybe even coming to a halt, though Cody decided he had to be imagining that. But there did seem no reason not to take a few minutes to search for water along the ridge where the mesquite was greener.

"We're turning in here!" he shouted to Mary, who still rode about ten yards ahead. "We're going to look for water among those trees!" He pointed to the trees and turned into the brush without waiting for a reply. The boy turned in behind him, and Cody guessed that Mary would too.

Cody was rapidly coming to an unsatisfying conclusion about the woman he had managed to rescue. As much as he was attracted to her, she didn't seem at all interested in him. Of course, she had seen to his wounds and nursed him, but she would have done that for anyone. He was somewhat chagrined at such a conclusion. Usually, he had little trouble attracting women— up to a certain point, anyway. But Mary seemed to have little interest in him . . . other than in his health. Well, he had been rejected by a few women before, and if rejection it turned out to be, he could handle it. Still. . . .

He picked their route carefully through the brush, but the tough, sharp-clawed branches tore at the steeldust's chest and at Cody's boots and thighs. He had chaps in his war bag, but he gave no thought to taking them out.

And finally the old mustanger turned out to be right. The water dribbled from between two rocks about five feet up the side of the slope and formed a small pool in a stone pan. When it overflowed the pan, it ran off into the mesquite and disappeared into the dry ground. Cody groaned as he dismounted. He filled the canteen and passed it first to Mary, who had come up to him and the boy. She took a long, grateful drink and passed it back. Cody gave it to the boy. Then he drank himself. Next the horses were led one at a time to drink from the little pool.

"I sure am hungry," the boy said.

"I have some jerky here," Cody answered, reaching into his saddlebag. When he pulled it out, he noticed that half of it was gone.

"I used some for broth last night," Mary explained. "Red Wind stopped so that I could feed you. Then Brad and I ate some this morning."

"I can't think of a better time to finish it off," Cody said, passing some to each of them.

"I've been wondering how you stayed in the saddle." Mary wasn't angry anymore, but she managed to show what she thought of his not taking her advice earlier. "All that blood you lost and nothing to eat—do all Rangers think they're so tough?"

He found out that he didn't mind the fussiness at all. In fact, he rather liked it, though what her purpose was confused him.

"Look!" Brad said. "Isn't that somebody riding in?"

"Into the brush!" Cody ordered, pulling out the Winchester and studying the advancing rider in the fast-fading twilight. Then the man waved and Cody relaxed, remembering the peasant clothes Red Wind had managed to come up with. "Never mind," he told the others. "It's our Indian friend."

Red Wind pulled up before them. His eyes went first to Cody. Then they quickly passed on to Mary.

"I was fearing that the Tofoyas had set another trap for you," Cody said.

"And I left you half dead in a travois," the Indian replied. "I found where you discarded it earlier. The Tofoyas found it too."

"How many are back there?" Cody asked.

"A dozen or more."

"They'll go into camp for the night, won't they?" Cody asked.

"No."

"What do you mean? They can't track us in the dark."

"They don't intend to. They've figured out

where we're going. They're heading straight for
my village."

"We'll have to beat them there and give some
warning," Cody said.

"The three of you could ride east. You could
be halfway home before the Tofoyas learn you're
not in the village. It's Mary whom Juan Tofoya
wants."

"What would happen to your people?" Mary
asked.

"I don't know," Red Wind said.

She turned to Cody. "I can shoot as well as
any man. Give me a gun and let's go with Red
Wind."

"What about Brad?" Cody asked.

"I can use a gun too," the boy said quietly.

He had more spunk than a boy should have,
and Cody patted his shoulder. "Let's hope it don't
come to that, son," he said. "But if it does, just
pour the lead into them."

"I would if I had a gun."

"Will these do?" Red Wind asked, producing
a Winchester that looked new and also a Colt
like the one around Cody's hips.

Mary reached for the rifle and Brad took the
six-gun.

"You might need these," Red Wind continued,
passing along two bandoliers heavy with cartridges. "This is for the pistol," he said, giving

the first to Brad. "And these are for the rifle," he added as he gave the other one to Mary.

"How did you come into those?" Cody asked.

"Their owner scouted too far ahead of the pack."

"Was his name Jesus?"

"It was—Jesus Garcia."

"You've done a mighty fine day's work," Cody said. "Maybe tomorrow we can even improve on it."

"I'd like nothing better."

"Are you two going to sit here talking while the Tofoyas beat us to the village?" Mary asked.

"An Amazon woman," Cody said.

"A fighting squaw," Red Wind agreed.

"But she's got a point. You take the lead and I'll bring up the rear."

Red Wind gave a shout that sounded a little like "ha" and slapped his knees to the side of his mount. The animal responded as if he'd been trained by an Indian. The others fell into place behind—Brad first, then Mary, and Cody bringing up the rear.

Cody was glad they had just given their mounts a rest, for the pace set by Red Wind was fast. He also noticed that Mary had hardly taken her eyes off Red Wind since the Comanche had rejoined them.

*   *   *

The ride was one that Mary would never forget. Red Wind set the pace, but he didn't push the horses wildly, regardless of what was at stake for him. Rather, he kept a pace suitable for the long haul, which ate up the miles but left the horses with a little in reserve.

They had begun the last leg of the ride just at twilight, when Red Wind joined them. During the first hour or so, the night seemed darker than it really was, because eyes accustomed to daylight must be given time to adjust to night.

But the almost total darkness didn't seem to bother Red Wind, Mary decided. As they continued to follow the hogback north, the ridge loomed more forbiddingly and steadily grew taller. Then it suddenly grew into a mountain.

They circled the mountain and entered a narrow pass that curled back west again. Tall cliffs rose up on each side, and Mary saw high above a slit of light where they seemed to end. Above that, a couple of stars seemed to wink at her. But the darkness in the pass was almost total, and the clatter of hooves on the stone drowned out all other sounds.

Red Wind continued to maneuver them through. Maybe he had traveled the route so often that he could feel his way. At the same time, he must have been able to communicate that familiarity to his mount, for the pace was hardly slowed though Mary could barely see her hand before her face.

Once beyond the pass they entered a valley. Taking a bearing by the North Star, Mary knew they were traveling northwest now. High peaks bordered the valley on each side, and after the darkness of the pass, the tall peaks seemed almost dazzling, even at night.

More stars came out, and their cold light glanced off the granite peaks like polish. Then, to her left on the western horizon, Mary saw the moon, its color strangely red. Soon the valley widened into a plain and they left the high peaks behind.

After they left the thin soil that had deadened the sound of their running horses, the pounding of the iron shoes beat a steady rhythm on the boulder-strewn surface, disturbing not only the valley but the night. But Mary knew that the noise made by their steady but desperate run didn't matter much. What did matter was that they reach the village before the comancheros and give warning of the attack. But even in the midst of the urgency of the race, she found herself thinking of the fate of those around her.

First, there was Brad. The change in him in just a few weeks was frightening. Mary had seen a new understanding of the world creep into his eyes. Before, his innocent horizons had ended at the mouth of Beaver Creek Canyon. He had now looked upon the remainder of the world, and he had been tested against the evil there. That look of total innocence would never appear in his eyes again, even though in years and size he remained but a slip of a boy.

How Brad felt about what had happened to him remained a mystery. Mary had been unable to get him to do much talking, which was another change, because before their capture, Brad had been something of a chatterer. Now there was a silence in him, and Mary could only hope that once they were safe again, the brother she had raised would revert to something of his former self. She would do everything she could to help him, and that thought determined her more than ever not to return to the place that would always be a reminder for Brad of what they had been through.

Then there was Cody Carson. She had to admit she liked the tall, rangy Texan. There was something about him that reminded her of most men she had known, though there was also much that was different about him. How she would ever repay her debt to him she didn't know. Without his persistence, she would never have escaped the horrors of being a captive of Juan Tofoya.

She sensed Cody's interest in her, and it

wasn't something that made her uneasy though she didn't reciprocate it. Actually, she had had little experience with men. Her only suitors had been two shy cowboys who rode for Charlie Goodnight. They had been too bashful to call on her alone and had always come together, as if to allow her a better opportunity to make up her mind between them. But she had known from the beginning that the only life she could expect from either of them was the one she already knew. She had had enough of that, and as she began to ignore them, they ceased calling on her.

The big Texan was no shy cowboy, but Mary could easily envision what a life with him would be like. He had mumbled while unconscious about the town of Mobeetie, and the woman who married Ranger Cody Carson would always be stuck in some such backwater town. She would spend most of her life waiting for him to be bushwhacked on some lonely trail while he was chasing badmen. No, though she owed Cody a lot, and he was obviously attracted to her, she would have nothing to do with such a life.

Surprisingly, her thoughts had been turning more and more to Red Wind. She had spent only a few hours with him, but that time had been intense. As her father had always said about war, a hundred years can be compressed into a minute if the action of it is right. Of course,

Amos Tate had meant the battles of war, but Mary felt that her time with Red Wind had been much like that.

They had fought together to save Cody's life by removing the bullet and stemming the flow of blood. Then they had worked desperately together to fashion the travois on which to haul him, afraid all the while that the comancheros would be down upon them. As Red Wind led them north, he had been as concerned for Cody as she was, as anxious to stop and feed him the broth that could save his life. She admired such loyalty.

During one of those stops, Red Wind had told her the story of his rescue by Cody. He hadn't exactly described what would have happened to him had he not been saved by the Ranger, but Mary, reading between the lines, gathered that he would have been tortured before he was killed. What drew her to him was Red Wind's great sense of debt to the Ranger, something she could certainly understand. Of course, the rescue was credit to Cody, but she had already known of his courage. What seemed more dramatic to Mary was Red Wind's loyalty and devotion to the man who had saved him. She wouldn't have expected that from what she knew of Comanches.

Her previous contacts with Indians had been

few, but here was a man who was a far cry from the Comanche savages in the stories of rape, murder, and pillage she had heard all her life. Here was a man of education and with sensibilities that were rare even in a white man. But there was more in him, and Mary found herself toying with the possibilities.

Might not Red Wind, under a different name, manage to make a place for himself in some civilized situation? He had the background of a schoolmaster, and she could see him teaching in an interesting town and enjoying a very nice existence. Maybe not in Texas or even in the West, but there was always the East.

Mary had often imagined what it would be like to live in a modern town in the East. Visitors could call every day if they had a mind to. There would be churches to attend...places to go where a woman naturally put on her best dress, and not for a stroll along Beaver Creek, where she would be grinned at by her father and Shorty when she returned. Suddenly, she saw herself helping Red Wind to make such a place for himself.

But it was far more than such a fantasy picture that had turned her thoughts toward Red Wind. There was something about him she couldn't quite fathom, a feeling she couldn't put into words because she didn't understand it. A woman with more experience might have had the same trouble, for it was something in the eyes of Red Wind that spoke of knowledge gleaned from a different heritage and experience. Her response was to something she felt was faintly primitive and wild, but she couldn't nail it down. Even as she considered it, she felt a new warmth begin to build inside her. There was something a little reckless in the feeling, and she felt her face burn in the darkness.

Soon after, they stopped in the shadow of a cliff to rest the horses. Solicitous of Cody, Red Wind asked if he wanted to dismount, but he declined. Then Red Wind offered upstretched hands to Mary. She lifted a leg over the cumbersome saddle and slid down to him. He caught her with hands beneath her arms and held her for a moment, her feet not touching the ground. Their faces were so near that she could feel his breath upon her cheek.

As he faced the west, the angry moon was reflected in his eyes, which seemed to increase the unknown quality that intrigued her. She felt as light as a feather between his hands, and she had a quick impression of his enormous physical power, a sense quite different from the educated schoolmaster image she had fashioned for him. She had the strongest feeling that he was about to kiss her, or was thinking about it, at least.

She caught a glimpse of Cody's face over Red Wind's shoulder. The night was too dark for her to read what was reflected there, but Mary could imagine it, and suddenly she was frightened. She couldn't have said whether it was because of what she knew was in Cody's face or the new and disturbing discovery she had just made about Red Wind. Maybe her reaction was a result of both.

"Put me down!" she commanded.

His reaction was instantaneous. He dropped her so quickly that her feet bounced her off the ground. When she caught her balance and looked at him, all she saw of Red Wind was his broad back as he walked away from her in the darkness. Her next look was at Cody. His face was turned away from her and toward Red Wind, whose white clothes disclosed his silhouette some thirty feet from where Mary stood. She had no idea what Cody thought of what had happened, but his stiffened posture seemed to tell her that his judgment had been harsh, though whether its object was she, or Red Wind, or maybe both of them, she couldn't tell.

Mary thought of walking out into the darkness where she could vaguely make out the white of Red Wind's peasant suit. She wanted to offer an apology, but when she tried to think of what to say, she was stumped. How could she explain something she had no understanding of? Better to sort things out before she spoke to him . . . if sort them out she could.

The silence between Mary and Cody was like a weight, and to break the spell, she glanced about for Brad. He stood now with his forehead pressed against the flank of his horse. He was so still as to seem asleep.

Mary walked over, turned him about, and held him against her. He didn't say anything, but put his arm about her waist. Was he frightened or just too tired to do anything else?

"Are you all right?" she asked.

"I'm fine."

"Are you sure?"

"I'm sure. Why wouldn't I be?"

There was something strange in the question, and Mary wondered if Brad had seen what had happened between her and Red Wind. If he had, what had he thought about it?

"These hosses are cooled down now, Red Wind. It's time to ride."

Cody's voice had a practical sound to it. Mary climbed upon the big roan as Red Wind strode back among them. He mounted without a look at anyone and sent his horse north into the darkness.

Chapter Seven

They climbed what appeared to be a molten lava slope that sapped what little strength was left in the horses. Even the steeldust slowed before the summit was reached.

Two spiny hogbacks of bluish granite guarded the pass on each side. Here and there small caves stared down upon the small party. A white bird of enormous size came from one cave and perched on its lip, eyeing the riders below before it took flight. Overhead, a pair of eagles seemed anchored in the sky as they rode a current of wind. Cody stared down into a small valley.

A lake banked against a medium-high cliff of gray stone. The surface of the water was glassy and very dark. Mist like blue smoke curled up from the smooth surface. Though the lake seemed tranquil enough, there was something unusual about it . . . the color of the water, or maybe the mist, which rose in faint swirls to disappear a few feet up.

To the east of the small lake was a stand of trees—oak, pine, and a few cottonwoods. The oaks formed the outermost circle, and beneath the edge of these, and facing the water over a sandy beach, were a dozen or so tepees. They formed a horseshoe that faced the lake. In the center of the half circle was a cooking fire whose smoke rose like a small funnel straight into the sky.

Two women worked about the fire, and a half dozen children played in the area. East of the trees, a herd of twenty or more horses grazed. Two half-grown boys, maybe the size and age of Brad, guarded the herd on barebacked ponies.

In all his life Cody had never witnessed a more peaceful scene. It would have passed for a photograph or a painting on a calendar. He sat with his hands folded about the horn of the saddle and drank it in with his eyes.

"It's beautiful," Mary murmured, her voice so low that Cody wondered if she didn't want Red Wind to hear her admiration.

"It is," Cody agreed. "Better still, I think we won the race. Nothing I see down there smacks of comancheros."

"They haven't come yet," Red Wind said.

He sat his horse just beyond the crest of the

ridge and seemed to enjoy the peaceful, pastoral scene as much as those who were seeing it for the first time. Even Brad seemed to rise out of his weary lethargy to enjoy the view. Red Wind seemed content to allow them a sustained look despite the danger behind them. Maybe he wanted to impress Mary, Cody thought, because the scene of the night before was deeply embedded in his mind, and had been strong in his thoughts ever since.

Cody had known from the beginning that Red Wind was in love with Mary. What he hadn't been prepared for was Mary's returning his interest. Cody's first reaction had been anger as he gazed down upon the two the night before. He held himself in check, however, when he saw that Mary was as involved in the relationship as Red Wind. Their faces had been so close that he thought their lips would touch. Then Mary had given her command.

Surprisingly, Cody's sympathy had been with Red Wind, and he had almost spoken a reprimand before he realized that what happened between Mary and Red Wind was of a personal nature and none of his affair. Part of Cody's anger was because he felt somewhat spurned, but how much was that and how much was due to the fact that Mary was a white woman and

Red Wind an Indian, Cody had no idea. He hadn't even tried to unravel his feelings.

Suddenly, Red Wind reached for his rifle, pointed the barrel into the sky, and squeezed off a shot. The two women by the fire and the children at play froze into statues. A moment later a half dozen men, two women, and more children poured from the tepees and from beneath the trees. The two boys guarding the horses were galvanized into action and started the herd toward the cover of the trees. Cody knew at once that the shot was a signal of danger. Then a rider shot from beneath the trees and galloped toward them up the slope.

They met him a few yards down the decline. The man was old and he wore thin white cotton pants and a sleeveless shirt. His shoes were cloth but fashioned in the style of moccasins. His gray hair hung to his shoulders. The small, dark eyes from the folds of wrinkled skin peered from Red Wind to the strangers.

The old man and Red Wind spoke briefly in their native tongue. Then Red Wind turned to the three whites behind him. "This is Prairie Walker," he said, indicating the old man facing them. "He will keep watch in the pass for the comancheros while we go down for some food. When we have eaten, we will reinforce him."

"Is there no other way into the valley?" Cody asked.

"There is another way in and out," Red Wind replied, "but it is a high climb and takes time. Even if the Tofoyas know of it, which I don't think they do, they're in too much of a hurry to take it. I think we can depend on them coming through here." He indicated the pass and the slope they had just climbed.

He gave a signal, and Prairie Walker sent his mount around them and up the slope. Cody watched till he disappeared over the crest. He hoped that the comancheros didn't show up until Red Wind sent up the reinforcements. One old man wouldn't be much help against a dozen or more well-armed bandits who were itching for plunder as well as a fight.

"Come," Red Wind said, and he led them down the slope. "Prairie Walker tells me the Apaches have returned west off the llano. Apparently, the comancheros scared them off, and we won't have to fight both of them."

"That's something," Cody agreed, though he wondered what difference a few Apaches thrown in might have made. Already, they faced what he considered impossible odds.

As they covered the rest of the short distance to the village, his mind toyed with the idea of what might have happened had he never entered the comanchero camp and cut Red Wind free. He would have found Mary and the boy soon enough. Of course, Red Wind had helped him get them away from the comancheros by providing the distraction, but he would have thought of something. Red Wind would be dead now, but that might have been more acceptable than the slaughter about to start.

Cody found himself considering another possibility. If Mary had never met Red Wind, would she have reacted differently to him and the way he felt about her? Maybe, but he had his doubts. Cody was surprised at how he had already managed to put his feelings for her into the past.

He felt different about the boy, however. A kid, he had stood up to having everyone and everything but his sister snatched from him. He had also faced up to being at the mercy of the meanest bunch of skunks that Cody could imagine. That the shock and the strain had worked mightily on Brad was obvious, but Cody had seen men who wouldn't have stood up under it as well.

During the night he had found himself thinking about hanging around and making sure that the boy made out all right. These were strange thoughts for a man who prided himself on being independent, but the boy might need a hand, depending on what happened between a certain unique Indian and a white woman with more courage than wisdom.

The small group of Indians made a circle about them when they pulled up before the tepees. Cody's first thought was a comparison between the people about him and the Indians he remembered from the reservations. There was little to compare. Here were healthy, normal, and curious people. He saw nothing of the beaten, whipped looks he remembered so well. These people weren't beggars. They were people who were responsible for themselves and took pride in the fact.

The men were old, much older than the women. All wore the same thin cotton suit that Prairie Walker had worn. The women wore sleeveless cotton dresses that reached well below their knees. The older children were dressed like the adults of their sex. The smaller children wore nothing at all.

Large or small, old or young, there was a similarity about them that seemed striking to Cody, not that they all looked like brothers and sisters, though that description seemed appropriate for the old men. All the faces were dark and tanned, as were legs and arms. They had dark eyes and even darker hair that fell to the shoulders of both men and women. The exception was the hair of the old men, which was from gray to snowy white.

The oldest man among them stepped forward. His face resembled a wrinkled prune, but in the midst of the deep crevices, small lively eyes peered out at the world.

His arms were almost fleshless, and the skin hung loosely on the bone. What struck Cody most were his legs. They were the most unusual physical attributes among a bewildering number of others. Proportionate to the old man's body, they were the longest legs that Cody had ever seen. There was no doubt in Cody's mind that he was looking at Man of Long Legs, the old chief of whom Red Wind had spoken so reverently.

Red Wind gave Man of Long Legs a signal and they spoke in Spanish.

"I bring bad news, Father," Red Wind said.

"I was told that the Apaches have returned to their homes in the West. Have they returned?" the old man asked.

"No, the danger is from the comancheros, the ones led by Juan Tofoya, of whom we have spoken before. He has led a second raid against the rancher who lived in the small canyon off the Palo Duro. This woman and boy are the daughter and son of that rancher. The comancheros took them captive."

"Ah," the old Indian said softly, and the dark little eyes glistened more brightly for a moment. He examined Mary first, but his eyes lingered longer on Brad. Then he switched his gaze to Cody.

"This man saved my life, Father," Red Wind said.

"How?"

"I was trailing the comancheros to make sure they passed the village by. Foolishly, I rode into their trap. This man slipped into their camp when they were sleeping and cut me loose. He is a great warrior of the Texas Rangers of whom I have heard you speak. I consider him my brother."

"I fought against the Rangers in Texas," the old man said. "They were fierce fighters. They used the fast-shooting little guns the white man wears against us." The old Indian was silent for a moment. Apparently, his mind was somewhere back in time, his thoughts on his many battles.

Cody still sat astride the steeldust. Now he lifted a leg and slid to the ground. He stood alongside the mare with a hand on the saddle horn for support, though he was pleasantly surprised at the absence of any pain in his back. He was also surprised at the strength he managed to muster.

The old man stepped toward Cody. He extended a hand that resembled a claw, and when Cody took it in his own, he felt the dry skin and bones.

"This man took a bullet from a comanchero's gun," Red Wind added from beside them.

Man of Long Legs, still shaking Cody's hand, said, "You are welcome in this village, Texas Ranger. Our women will give you food, and we will provide you a place to rest if you are weak."

"This white man's name is Cody Carson, Father," Red Wind said. "He will fight the comancheros with us despite the bullet he took. The woman, too, can use a gun. I have been told she could outshoot the white men who raised her but are now dead. She has come to fight as well. And the boy too."

"We will have need of their guns," the old man said, dropping Cody's hand and stepping back. "This Tofoya is an evil man. I knew his father, a man who put water in the whiskey he sold the Comanches though we gave him many of the finest skins in return."

"I thank the chief," Cody said haltingly in Spanish. "We have great friendship for Red Wind and his people, and we will fight to defend this village. I shall tell my own chief back in Mobeetie of the words you have spoken about the Rangers. He fought against the Comanches, and I have heard him speak many times of their courage and bravery and superb horsemen."

The old man was pleased at the praise, and he studied Cody even more intently for a moment. Then he said, "Our men are old, with the exception of Red Wind, whom I have made my son. And with the exception of Red Wind, we will all be dead before most of our children reach the age of marriage. When he came among us, Red Wind brought us hope of survival. We owe you much obligation for his rescue. He is our war chief. You and he will fight well in this battle, and you will fight it together. But before you fight, you must eat."

He clapped his hands and the two women at the cooking fire brought them bowls of steaming stew. Cody, Mary, and Brad ate where they stood, dipping into the bowls with their fingers, since nothing else was offered. The lumps of meat that Cody fished out were tasty, though he had no idea what they were. The vegetables could have been tomatoes and okra.

Red Wind and Man of Long Legs had stepped apart, and Cody watched them from the corner of his eye. He also heard the murmur of their talk, but they no longer spoke in Spanish, which made him a little nervous. Then Red Wind rejoined them, saying, "The plan is made."

"Tell me about it," Cody said.

Red Wind hesitated before he spoke, and his eyes showed some nervousness. "Except for Man of Long Legs, the men of the village and I will meet the comancheros in the pass." He paused and gave Cody another nervous look.

"Where will *I* be?" Cody asked.

"You and Man of Long Legs will guard the village. You will make the last stand if the Tofoyas get through the pass."

"I think I could be of more use in the pass," Cody said. He wondered why he was to be left in the village, and thought of a couple of reasons. Maybe Red Wind felt he was still too weak from loss of blood to stand up to the comancheros. Maybe Red Wind, still thinking there was competition between them for Mary's attention, wanted to hog the glory. That thought almost brought a smile to Cody's lips. This educated Indian didn't know he had already won the battle between them, if there had even been a battle.

"Man of Long Legs requests that you stay and fight with him," Red Wind said, almost apologetically. "He says he has always hated the Texans, and he now finds himself sorry for that. He wants the honor of fighting alongside one to erase all those bad feelings. Will you fight with him from here, Cody? I fear he might follow us into the pass if you go with us. And there is another reason. You would not be a Ranger if you were not very good with that rifle. Do you see that slope? One man could cut down a dozen attackers before they reached the village. You will stand between the women and the children if they get past us. You will be their only hope."

"I will fight here with Man of Long Legs," Cody said, knowing there was no way he could refuse a request worded in such a way.

The four old men who had recently been in the group surrounding Red Wind and the white visitors had disappeared. Now they came from beneath the trees. All four were mounted and one led an extra horse. Red Wind saw them, but before joining them, he turned to Mary and said, "I apologize for what I did last evening. You had every right to be offended."

Cody thought that he sounded as prim as a New England preacher he had once heard in Dallas. He looked at Mary and saw the struggle in her face. It lasted too long, and Red Wind turned and walked to the spare horse. Grabbing a handful of mane, he swung himself up in the fashion Cody had admired that first night in the ravine. He had never seen a man mount a horse so gracefully.

"Wait!" Mary shouted, but if Red Wind heard her, he gave no sign.

"I can't let him get killed before I tell him how

I feel," she said. Running to the big roan who was still unsaddled, she climbed up and sent the animal after the small band of Indians.

Cody was surprised by her wild ride up the slope, and turning to Brad, he said, "I think you have an unpredictable sister."

"Will she marry him, do you think?" Brad asked.

"I don't know," Cody answered. "How'd you feel about it if she did?"

"I don't want to stay out here in the desert," he said.

"How would you like to come to Mobeetie... if that meeting up there works out?"

Cody referred to Mary and Red Wind, who, with their mounts close together, had been left behind by the other Indians. From what he could tell Mary was doing most of the talking. Beside him, Brad watched the couple just as closely.

"Mary has always said I should go to school," Brad said finally. "Is there a school in Mobeetie?"

"A small one, but the teacher is said to be a good one."

"We'll talk to my sister about it... if she can get her mind off that Indian long enough."

Cody wasn't sure he liked Brad's words and tone, but he excused them. "You come with me,"

Cody said. "I think it's time we looked around for a place to shoot from."

There was no sign of an Indian anywhere. Then, from behind a line of boulders beneath the oaks, he saw Man of Long Legs. The old man was signaling for Cody and Brad to join him, which they did. The boulders had obviously been arranged for just such use, and Cody settled down beside the old Indian, with Brad on his other side. All three watched as Mary rode back down the slope. Her return was much slower than her ride up, and Cody thought he saw rejection in her face as she dismounted and led the roan beneath the trees.

After taking the bandolier of bullets from the saddle, she took a place behind a rock next to her brother. No one asked her what had happened between her and Red Wind, and she didn't volunteer anything.

The pass through which the comancheros would come was shaped like a funnel. Its wide end was to the east and its narrow point ended at the crest of the slope that overlooked the valley. The formation offered the defenders two advantages, or so it seemed to Red Wind.

The comancheros would be riding uphill on tired horses. Maybe the slope would slow them down even more, thus making them easier targets. Then the narrowing pass would confine them and compress them into a compact group more vulnerable as targets. At a certain point, Juan Tofoya's men would be riding directly into the firepower of the six Indians set to stop their advance.

With the five old warriors grouped about him, Red Wind surveyed the positions from which they would fight. His heart warmed at the respect they showed him, and there wasn't one among them who didn't seem something of a father to him. And now some of them, maybe all, including himself, would die.

They had the appearance of brothers as they grouped about him. Their dark, wrinkled faces and their black, deeply recessed eyes suggested brotherhood. Their names ran through his mind, and they were like the roll call of an almost vanished Comanche culture—Many Coyotes, Blue Fox, Prairie Walker, Mountain Fire, and Dog Barking. They were names that spoke of the man's place in nature and among his people. Descriptive and meaningful names were dying out among reservation Indians. Maybe that was because the Comanche life had been killed when the plains were wrested from them and they were forced onto the few acres allowed them. Now Comanche mothers and fathers gave their children the white man's names, often from the white man's Bible, and at the urgings of the missionaries. Such names denied the dignity of Comanche culture and traditions, and made those who bore them ashamed of what they had been.

So Red Wind looked about at the faces of the very remnants of a race, and the fear that he might now be looking upon their likes for the last time in his life was like a heavy hand that squeezed his heart. They had led unique lives, and the world would never know such men again.

"My fathers," he said, "the time has come when we are called upon to lay down our lives to protect this small corner of what remains true Comanche earth. We must not let those who would destroy what is left of us get past this point. Comanches will never ride the plains again. We will never pitch our tepees beneath the willows along the many rivers that split its grassy meadows. Nor will we sleep with the songs of the pines, the cottonwoods, and the willows in our ears. Nor will we ever again find refuge from the seasons of blowing snow in the wild Palo Duro. We few here cannot stand against the tide that swept us from our land, but it is left for us to protect what is left."

Red Wind stopped and looked into their ancient faces, and he knew that his words had touched them. The gleam in their old eyes seemed a little brighter, their backs a little straighter, and their grip on their rifles was the grip of younger men.

"Your words make warriors out of us, our son," Dog Barking said. "We will keep the comancheros from the village, and when we have won a victory, we will celebrate with a great feast. Blue Fox himself, who is the greatest storyteller among us, will choose the words that will add this fight to the list of other Comanche battles. Mountain Fire will compose a song, and he will use the words you have spoken to us here, for even his great skill cannot surpass what you have said."

There were murmurs of agreement from the other four, and Red Wind knew he had fulfilled one of the duties of a Comanche war chief: He had prepared the spirit of those he led for battle. Now he must tell them of the strategy he had devised.

He pointed to the boulders that lined both sides of the pass. "Blue Fox and Prairie Walker will take up positions behind those rocks," he said. "Mountain Fire and Dog Barking will fire from behind the rocks opposite them. Many Coyotes and I will fight from here." He indicated a line of sawtooth rock that blocked the center of the pass that was just before them and less than twenty yards from the summit overlooking the valley. Then, at his signal, the old warriors walked briskly to their positions.

Until he was settled into his position beside Many Coyotes, Red Wind had spared no time to assess what had happened between Mary and himself a few minutes before. He had not wanted to hear her words, but she had practically blocked his path with the big roan, and she had threatened to follow him into the pass if he didn't listen. What she had said was such a shock that he had lost some of her words, but he remembered their import well enough.

"What happened last night was none of your fault," she had begun. "I confess I was afraid, but I was frightened of what I felt inside myself, and not from being held there so close to you. I know we haven't much time, and what I am about to say may shame me in your eyes, but I cannot let you ride away from me without telling you how I feel. I love you, Red Wind, and I think you love me too. Just tell me if that's true before I make a bigger fool of myself than maybe I already have."

Her words had been a thunderbolt to his heart. They seemed to explode in the very air about him, shattering the facade behind which he had learned to hide his Indian self from all whites. Until that moment he had never believed a red man could ever hear those words from a white woman, especially one so beautiful as the one who now spoke them to him. When he spoke, he spoke as an Indian, the words coming from his Indian heritage, something he had never done before with a white, not even the Texas Ranger who had snatched him from the hands of Jesus Garcia, Juan Tofoya's torturer.

"Your words strike my heart like the rainstorm that descends upon the driest meadow, waters its grass and trees, and never leaves though surely the years do gentle it some. I do love you, Mary Tate, but I do not believe this is a union that will ever come to be... *can* ever come to be."

She had reached a hand out to rest it upon his own, and the feel of that hand was as warm as a torch. Looking into her eyes, he had seen the courage that had brought her up the hill to catch him. Then she had asked the question he had known would come:

"Why, Red Wind? Why can't it be if we love each other?"

"I am an Indian," he had said. "I have found that there is no place in the white man's world for me, just as there is no place in the Indian world for me except that village there." He had indicated the half circle of tepees below them with a sweep of his hand.

"I have a plan," she had said. "We will go East. You are an educated man and well qualified to teach. There are always jobs for well-qualified teachers."

"Will I go by the name of Red Wind when I apply?"

"I have heard it said that Indians take different names when they attend the Indian school. What name did you choose?"

"James Travers."

"I like that name. It has an English sound. You will introduce yourself as James Travers, though you will not lie about who you are or where you were trained."

He had been tempted, but he knew that the life she offered would be no more than an extension of the white man's world he had fled when he left the school in Pennsylvania and returned to Oklahoma Territory. Even with her beside him, he would never be able to fit back into such a world.

"It would never work," he had said. "We would hate each other within a year." And he recognized he was speaking not as a Comanche then but as a white man.

She hadn't argued, but she wasn't giving up. "There is one other choice."

"What?"

"We can rebuild the ranch in Beaver Creek

Canyon. It belongs to Brad and me now. We can live there, like the Comanches always did until a few years ago."

Until the white man took it from us, he had almost said, but he squelched the words. Her words held an offer that he had thought would never be made to a Comanche, the chance to live again in their ancestral winter home. It was something he couldn't reject out of hand, and he said, "We will speak of this later."

He had watched her ride back into the village and beneath the trees. Then he had turned his mount and joined the old warriors in the pass.

Chapter Eight

The silence beyond the summit of the pass was a torture for Cody. He had never been so near a just fight without taking a hand in it. He found himself regretting his agreement to stay behind, and several times he considered retrieving the steeldust from the trees and joining Red Wind in the pass. What deterred him was the sight of Man of Long Legs taking a rifle into his hands. Cody had seen the hands of old men tremble with palsy before, but never so badly as the hands of the old chief.

Cody was sure then that the old man's condition was why Red Wind had left him in the village in the first place. The impressive words that Red Wind had spoken to Cody, of the old chief's honor to fight alongside one of his old foes, had been bunkum. And Cody found himself wondering about the story Red Wind must have made up to keep the old chief behind. No doubt, it would have been something to the effect that the Texas Ranger would find great honor in staying behind to fight beside Man of Long Legs as they defended the village together. He had to smile at Red Wind's deception. Here was a clever Comanche who carried in his head a whole bag full of tricks.

Cody had been very much aware of Mary's presence since her return. She had chosen a position that put Brad between them, but Cody had stolen a few glances at her. He would have loved to know what had passed between her and Red Wind to send her down the slope with such a look of rejection on her face. Surely, it wasn't because she had found that Red Wind didn't love her. Cody would have bet the steeldust that the Indian did.

It was Mary who made the choice to talk. "I suppose you're curious," she said, her voice strong and defiant.

"None of my business," he answered. "Last time I looked you were a grown woman. You don't have to explain anything to anyone if it's your decision not to."

As Brad rose from his crouch behind the line of rocks, Cody pushed him down again. The force of his hand was enough to silence whatever the boy had been about to say.

"I told him I loved him . . . that I would marry him if he was sure he loved me too."

"Will you live with him here in the village?" Cody asked.

"I offered to go East with him where he could teach school. He went by the name of James Travers when he was a student. That's a good name for a schoolteacher. Of course, we would never try to hide who he really is."

"Sounds like a sensible plan."

But there obviously had been some hesitation on Red Wind's part, or Mary wouldn't still be wearing the look of rejection. But Cody still felt barred from asking what had been Red Wind's response. Such a personal matter should be shared only if a participant volunteered it.

"He turned that idea down," she said.

"He doesn't love you, then?" Cody asked despite his Texas upbringing.

"Oh, yes, he does! But he said it wouldn't work."

Cody could have given a dozen reasons why it wouldn't. His respect for Red Wind grew even more, because such an offer must have tempted him greatly if his ardor burned as hotly for Mary as Cody believed it did.

"I made him another offer," she said. "I proposed that we live on the ranch and rebuild it together."

"I would think he jumped at that. I get the impression the Palo Duro means a lot to him. He would get to do what most Comanches would give an arm for, return to a place almost sacred to them."

"He said we would talk about it later," Mary answered.

But there was no joy in her words. Either she didn't expect Red Wind to live through the battle in the pass, or she expected him to refuse the offer. Whichever it was, Cody found himself feeling sad for her. It had cost her plenty to ride after Red Wind as she had.

"We *could* rebuild the ranch," she said then, as if to convince herself that the idea offered more than just a trifle of hope.

"You never spoke as if living there was something you wanted to do," Cody replied. "I recall you saying how important it was for you and Brad to get away so he could go to school. Maybe this is something you should discuss with him."

Cody realized suddenly that he wasn't raising the point for Brad's benefit alone. He had been sure that his own interest in Mary had died a-borning when he saw her fascination with Red Wind. Now he realized that some of that feeling still lurked within him. He wondered how he would feel if for some reason Red Wind turned her down. Or, worse, if Red Wind did not survive the battle in the pass. Would he have a chance with her then? Would he *want* a chance?

His mention of Brad had silenced her for a while. Finally she said, "Brad has always agreed with me. He'll do what I want him to do."

"Ask him."

But the boy didn't wait for her question. "I want to go to Mobeetie with Cody!" he yelled. "I don't want to live on no ranch with an Indian! I want to go to school, like you always said I should!"

The outburst left Mary speechless for a moment. Then she turned on Cody and cried, "You put that idea into his head, didn't you? You did it for spite!"

"Actually, I think *you* did it, a long time before me and the boy ever met. I did offer to look after him if you decided to tie the knot with Red Wind, which you have. I told him of the schoolmaster in Mobeetie, who is a good man though he may drink a little too much at times. Brad said he would have to talk it over with you, but my offer stands."

"I'm going!" Brad yelled.

"Might be best all around, considering the way he feels," Cody told Mary.

She was hurt, and Cody could see it, and he remembered she had been the only mother the boy had known. But in the lives of most people there were crossroads, a time and place to make choices. The time had come when Mary Tate would have to choose.

"I never knew you would feel so strongly," she said to Brad. Then she turned to Cody. "Pa and Shorty hated Indians, especially Comanches, because they fought against them so long."

"They were part of his life too," Cody said.

"Tell me I can go!" Brad demanded.

Mary was silent for a while. Then she said, "We'll see . . . if we live through this."

It was a very sound qualification, Cody thought, for if the comancheros came in force, there was every chance they wouldn't.

Red Wind and Many Coyotes crouched behind the sawtooth rocks. Red Wind's eyes and ears were focused on the wide eastern end of the pass, but there was still no sign of Juan Tofoya and his men. His mind drifted back to the incident that had finally sent him south in search of the Comanches.

Before that episode, he had believed that the gulf between a red man and a white woman could not be so wide. While in the enlightened environment of the Indian school with its white teachers, some of them missionaries, he had thought there was no chasm at all. Many young men in the school, including he, danced with white girls at town socials. Such a naive belief came to an abrupt end when he returned to the reservation. What happened there still brought a burn of anger to his face, and a sense of shame at what he was, and his helplessness to deny the shame.

He had been hunting rabbits when it happened. He came upon a girl from nearby Fort Sill who was out riding, a custom not unusual among Fort Sill girls, but generally they stayed closer in. This one had ridden farther, however, and her mount's cinch had broken. Red Wind stopped to offer his help, which she had accepted gratefully.

With his knife and some of the string he used for setting rabbit snares, he had stitched the broken ends of the cinch strap back together. "That should get you back to the fort," he told her. "But you should go slow."

She had stood beside him as he repaired the cinch, holding the ends of the leather together as he made the stitches. Once or twice her hair had brushed his face. Their hands had touched, and he had been pleasantly aware of her perfume. When the repair was finished, he resaddled her mount.

"Thank you," she said, extending a hand for

a shake. "What's your name, so I can tell my father you came to my rescue?"

He almost said James Travers before answering quickly, "It's Red Wind, but there is no need to mention anything so insignificant to your father."

He might have asked her name, for her hand was still in his as he prepared to help her mount. Then two uniformed men rode from the trees, one a sergeant and the other a captain. As they galloped toward them, he dropped the girl's hand guiltily.

"Father! This is Red Wind!" the girl cried at the two men bearing down on them. "He repaired the broken cinch!"

The panic in her voice suggested that not only Red Wind but she herself had something to fear. Red Wind might have run had he not been frozen by fear beside the horse.

When the captain pulled up, he lashed out with his riding whip, wrapping the plaited end across Red Wind's skull. From there it traveled down to his face and his neck with successive lashes. The leather plait ate into Red Wind's skin as if it were hungry for his blood.

He might have fought back, but the sergeant had pulled a pistol, and a gleam in the man's eyes told Red Wind that the slightest provocation would make him fire. Of course, a report would have been filed, relating how the sergeant and the captain had arrived on the scene in time to prevent an assault on the girl. The report would have been signed by them all, including the girl.

"That should teach you to mess with a white girl, Indian!" the father shouted. He said a great many other things, most of which Red Wind had managed to put from his mind.

With the bite of the whip still stinging, Red Wind had watched them ride away. That was the first time he had known for sure that he couldn't live on the reservation and maintain his self-respect, and a week later he rode south to search for the Comanches rumored to still live on the Llano Estacado.

Contentment and peace had been his then... until he saw Mary Tate. He had first seen her two days after her capture by the comancheros, who, having raided the ranch, were riding west into the desert. He knew what was in store for her, and his mind had toyed with a rescue.

With that in mind, he had followed the comancheros to their camp, but there was no chance to even get near the white woman, much less get her away from the comancheros. Finally, he rode north to the village, but he knew he would return.

On his return he found the spot on the ridge

overlooking the building where the woman and the boy were kept. He saw her clearly when she went out for a walk. With that close look into her face, he was stirred even more deeply. He returned several times, but could come up with no plan to get her and the boy out.

For reasons Red Wind hadn't quite figured out, he had wanted to tell Cody the whole story, just as Red Wind had retraced it in his mind. Why he had wanted to do that, Red Wind had still to figure out. What good would it have done to tell of the white girl and the beating? Or of how he had followed the comancheros because he was attracted to the white women they had captured? And what would Cody have thought of his returning time after time to the willow on the ridge without doing anything to free Mary?

But he knew why he had not spoken to Cody. He hadn't wanted Cody to know that Red Wind, the Comanche war chief, had been whipped by a white man like a thief, had stood with bowed head and been punished for fear of being shot. Red Wind had never even confessed so much to Man of Long Legs. Certainly, he didn't want Cody to know that he had submitted to such indignity. And yet. . . .

He hadn't told the Texan how he felt about Mary Tate for obvious reasons. Cody would have resented it, just as the captain at Fort Sill had resented what he had thought were Red Wind's advances toward his daughter. If he had seen such a look in Cody's eyes, Red Wind would have suffered all the old feelings of inferiority that he had been shaking loose in the desert.

But if he'd been afraid of Cody's knowing any of those things, had he really conquered any of the old shame? Suddenly, Red Wind felt almost exactly as on the day of the whipping. He hadn't made any progress at all. He was still a white-educated, reservation Indian with no idea at all of who he really was.

"You think deep thoughts, my son," Many Coyotes said.

Red Wind twisted about to face the old warrior. "They are the thoughts that brought me to the llano, old father. They are not thoughts to be shared at such a time. I will put them from my head and think of the victory we will share this day."

But Many Coyotes was not to be put off so easily. "You think of the white woman," he said. "I once picked a plum from a white man's orchard. It was even sweeter than the wild ones, but it would have grown nowhere else but in that garden with the white man to tend it. I have known the wild plum to be transplanted into a garden, but never the other way around."

Many Coyotes spoke in a parable, but his meaning was clear. He had told Red Wind that Mary would never be happy in the village, that if he took her as his wife, he should live with her in her own land among her own people. Red Wind almost told the old man of her offer to live with him in the Palo Duro. But he didn't.

With the exception of Man of Long Legs, who had adopted him into the village, Many Coyotes was Red Wind's favorite among the old warriors. It was Many Coyotes who had spent the most time teaching him to be a Comanche. A grown man when he came to the village, Red Wind had been more ignorant than the children of the traditions and customs of his people.

Many Coyotes had taken Red Wind's education upon himself. Night after night the old man sat beside the lake in the moonlight as the water lapped gently at the thin sand, and he taught Red Wind the history of the Comanche from the time they had drifted onto the southern plains from the mountains to the north. The story of the coming of the horse was included, and how the split between the Kiowas, close brothers of the Comanches, had come about.

"They come," Many Coyotes now said, bringing Red Wind back from reverie.

And Red Wind knew that the time of thought had ended. Now the time for what every true Comanche dreamed of had arrived. The battle would now come riding down the pass.

Chapter Nine

Red Wind focused on the wide entrance to the pass, and finally he saw them. They were just at the foot of the slope and coming on strong. As the incline became steeper, they slowed, and Red Wind could count them. They were fifteen, and they looked like an army as they spread out across the pass.

Apparently, they knew well where they were, for they rode with rifles ready, the sun glinting off the barrels and off the bullet-laden bandoliers about every rider's shoulders. The wind that whistled down the pass had swept the wide sombreros from the heads of many. Their black hair, wet with sweat, caught the sun as well. Red Wind, whose eyesight was that of an eagle, could already see their faces, the hard faces of cruel men eager for a fight and for plunder. They were a fearsome sight, and the folly of standing against them with only five old men struck Red

Wind like a blow to the heart. But he had no choice but to wait and face them.

No Comanche war chief ever told his warriors when to begin the attack upon an enemy. That was a judgment left to each warrior. Red Wind, too, had refrained from such instructions, for the theory of equality permeated every facet of Comanche life.

But one thing Red Wind did know, which gave him confidence that no shot would be fired prematurely and ruin the surprise. Every man who waited with him had been a warrior for more years than Red Wind had lived. The old men were far wiser in the ways of war than he would ever be. Instinctively, each would know when to open the attack.

He turned for a final look at Many Coyotes. The old warrior seemed to have shed twenty years. The thirst for battle had come into his body and turned it young again. His eyes had the gleam of a predator hawk as he stared at the riders approaching up the pass. Red Wind felt his own emotions surge, inspired by the fever that possessed Many Coyotes. As those feelings soared and sang inside him, Red Wind was confident that he knew at last what it was to be a Comanche, and he cast away the confusions brought on by years in the white man's school. No longer did he stand with a foot in two different worlds, split apart and torn between them. This battle, even before it began, had made him one with his people at last.

The din of pounding hooves was like the rumble of approaching thunder. It would reach well into the valley where the women and the children waited for the outcome. Mary waited there too, and the thought of her was like something alien to Red Wind, who only minutes before would have sworn that the most important thing in the world was to possess her. Now that thought hardly mattered to him at all. If he survived the battle, he now knew that he would send her back across the llano into the world that Juan Tofoya had wrenched her from. And if she rode at the side of any man, she would ride beside the big Texan who had come into a country he did not know for a woman he had never met. The two white people riding back together seemed most fitting and appropriate to Red Wind, the Comanche war chief.

Now the heavy grunt of struggling horses added to the approaching din. The Tofoya brothers were in the lead, and they sat their horses in the arrogant way of men who knew that nothing would stand before them and their ambitions. They were still too far away for Red Wind to tell who was who. From this distance, they resembled two peas from the same pod, and Red

Wind took aim at one because the horse he rode was white.

But the first shot came from the rocks along the south cliff, either from the rifle of Blue Fox or Prairie Walker. Then the battle was joined in earnest as both rifles from the line of rocks opened up, accompanied by the twin barks of the rifles of Mountain Fire and Dog Barking. Even Many Coyotes' rifle exploded in a belch of flame, bullet, and lead before Red Wind squeezed off his first shot. A fire he had never known before raced through his veins when he finally did pull the trigger and then saw the Tofoya in his sights go down.

For the first few moments chaos reigned among Tofoya's men. The screams of dying horses joined the din of battle, and Red Wind could see them go down, could see their struggles to be up again. And there were dead and dying men, though their yells seemed less tragic than the screams of the horses as they went down.

But the comancheros didn't fold. Nor did they flee back down the pass as Red Wind had secretly hoped that they would. Instead, they suddenly split into three groups at the orders of the Tofoya who was still in the saddle. One group charged the rocks that hid Blue Fox and Prairie Walker. Another rode for the boulders from behind which Mountain Fire and Dog Barking fought. The third, led by whichever Tofoya still rode, charged the sawtooth rocks.

Bullet after bullet shattered on the rocks and ricocheted across the pass. The smoke from the battle floated up the cliffs and resembled the low clouds that Red Wind had sometimes seen pass through. The smell of burned powder was strong in his nostrils. The barrel of the rifle was almost too hot for his hands.

Then Many Coyotes took a bullet and Red Wind almost threw his rifle aside to go to the old man. But the old warrior stopped him. A single look from the old man's eyes told Red Wind what to do, and the war chief who till this battle had never felt himself to be one turned his gun again on the party led by Tofoya.

As he fired he saw from the corners of his eyes how hopeless was the situation of the old warriors among the rocks. The comancheros were already upon them, firing almost straight down upon them from the backs of their mounts. But the four old warriors were giving a good account of themselves. Many dead horses and men who had not made it into the rocks lay sprawled before them.

Red Wind shot another rider from the saddle, which left four charging after Tofoya. He downed another, and then tried to hit Tofoya, hoping that killing him might turn the others back. When they were almost upon him, he stood up for better aim. Bullets from Tofoya's six-gun made a target of his chest and sent him staggering back. Then Tofoya's horse seemed to rise up and fly over the sawtooth rocks, striking Red Wind's bullet-ridden body head-on.

Red Wind landed with his face toward Many Coyotes, who lay across a rock. As he left this world, the young war chief's last thoughts were of this old man who had spun the history of the Comanches so magically in the moonlight for him . . . and, finally, to ponder why he had not painted and dressed himself properly for this last fight.

The clamor of battle from the pass echoed over the valley. Any lull in the explosions was filled with shrieks of falling and dying horses, a sound that had always rattled Cody's nerves to their very tips.

To help fill the hard moments of waiting, Cody focused his attention on the people about him. The antics of the old chief, Man of Long Legs, drew him first. Unable to sit behind the barricade, the old man had begun to dance in a slow, methodical way, raising his knees as high toward his chest as he could manage, and advancing in a circle that took him from the cover of the rocks and trees and into the sunshine. As he danced, he chanted a song in a high, thin, quavering voice that sent chills along Cody's spine.

Cody had no idea of the message of the song or dance, but he did know that it was meant not only to bolster the courage of the old chief but also to offer hope to the women and children hidden among the trees. Cody suspected the song and the dance might be an appeal to the Indian spirits for the success of the warriors beyond the pass. As Cody considered this thought, the song suddenly took on a more significant meaning for him and he could hear in the quavering old voice the echo of some ancient force now in its death throes, of a primal vitality that now faced extinction. The thought was so disturbing that he turned from the old chief and his faltering dance and song to Mary.

She sat rigidly behind the barricade, and her stiff, straight body seemed to consume as much energy as the old man's dancing. Her face was pale, and Cody could see a pulsing vein in her neck. She might have fared better during the wait had she joined the old man in his dance.

But for the first time, Cody thought he might have some understanding of why this woman, the daughter of a Texas rancher who had spent his early life killing Comanches, had been deeply touched by her contact with Red Wind.

She had sensed the mystery and excitement of something unknown, just as Cody himself had heard it in the old man's song. Whatever it was, it didn't seem so strange as it once might have to him. In fact, something in the old man's song seemed almost familiar. Maybe the primitive chant stirred something in the soul of every man. Maybe even white men had once possessed such feelings in the distant past.

Mary stood up suddenly, and Cody decided she might have taken the strain of what was happening beyond the hill as long as she could. She was a headstrong woman, and the idea occurred to Cody that she might be about to ride into the pass and see for herself what was happening. He was prepared to stop her if she tried. Then he realized that her reaction was due to a change in the explosions beyond the ridge. They seemed to be dying down a bit.

The boy was the quietest. He sat behind the barricade with his eyes glued to the summit, and holding the six-gun and the bandolier of bullets that Red Wind had given him. But Cody knew that a restful and quiet spirit was not what kept the boy so seemingly composed. He was beginning to know Brad, and something in the boy's features suggested just the opposite. In fact, there was something about the set of his face that seemed as old as the dancing Indian.

Cody recognized the look of a human being whose innocence had been violated by a dreadful shock, and he wondered again just what the boy had been subjected to. Whatever it was, it might stay buried within him for years to come, if not forever. But though the boy might never again be the innocent stripling who had been dragged from the Beaver Creek Canyon ranch, he deserved a chance to shed as much of the experience he had been through as he could. If he was forced to live and work on a ranch with an Indian he hated, even though that Indian was Red Wind, the boy might never have that chance. Even if he had to fight the sister, Cody made up his mind that Brad would be offered something different.

Next, Cody turned his thoughts to the women and children of the village, who were hiding in the trees. From time to time he heard a child ask what was an obvious question, though it was spoken in the Comanche tongue and he didn't understand it. Every girl, woman, and boy back there could have only one thing on their mind: *What will happen to me if the comancheros fight their way into the village?*

Then the clamor, which had been one long and sustained explosion, finally ceased. One way or another, in victory or in defeat for the Comanches, the battle was ended. Gluing his eyes to the summit, Cody waited to see who would appear. The wait was brief, and he recognized one of the Tofoyas by the big sombrero whose band was decorated by the silver conchas he remembered, and which now winked down at him as the sun bounced off the metal. Four other riders followed close behind.

The distance was too far for accurate shooting, but Cody, long impatient, took a shot anyway, lifting the Winchester to his shoulder and trying for the leader, whom he now recognized as Juan, the older of the brothers. The sun was in his face, and the downward plunging horse did not help. The first two shots missed, but the third shot knocked the rider directly behind Tofoya from his horse.

Cody continued firing, and from the corner of his eye he saw Brad join in. Beyond the boy, Mary was again crouched behind the barricade. She had the rifle to her shoulder and wore a determined look as she blasted away.

Only Man of Long Legs did not join in the fight. The chief still circled in his old man's dance, singing his songs with his eyes cast toward heaven. Whether the old chief knew the outcome of the battle in the pass, Cody could not have said. He seemed to know, however, though there had been no pause in the dance or song.

Maybe the old Comanche had divined the re-

sults, and his dance had now become one of piti-
ful defiance against the castrophe that was
about to finish engulfing the rest of his people.
If that were the case, to die singing and dancing
for something passing into extinction was as
good a way to die as any. Cody didn't even try
to get the old man's attention and urge him to
retreat behind the barricade. Instead, he
squeezed off shot after shot at Juan Tofoya, who
seemed to have as many lives as a cat.

Bullets zinged off the barricade and ricocheted
across the valley, screaming as they cut the
wind. The thunder from exploding guns cracked
flatly against the gray cliff over the lake, rolled
back to hit the trees, and then repeated the pro-
cess over again. The horses of two more comancheros went down, and their riders
somersaulted down the slope, leaving their
fallen animals behind. Both men lay still where
they stopped their roll.

Now only two riders were left—Juan Tofoya
and a companion. Both men defied death until
they were within twenty yards of the barricade.
Then the man who rode behind Tofoya seemed
to climb the air. His hands, reaching for something that maybe only he could see, fought
empty space. Then the horse stumbled and the
bandit was flung head forward into the barricade. After that, he did not move.

Juan Tofoya must have known that only he was left, but he didn't hesitate, possibly because he knew there could be no turning back. Instead, he sent his horse straight for the Texas Ranger, hoping to do to him what he had done to the Indian in the pass.

There was just barely time for Cody to get off a shot while the bandit chief lifted his horse upright in a head-on assault. The bullet missed its mark, and Cody barely had time to duck behind the rock and miss the flying hooves. But as Tofoya's booted foot flashed past his face, he reached out and caught it. Cody was yanked from the ground, but he held on, bringing Tofoya crashing down on top of him.

Cody landed on his back, and he heard the swoosh of his breath leave his body as Tofoya landed squarely atop his belly. For a long and eternal moment he couldn't breathe. He was aware of two things that followed . . . the rush of air into his lungs at last and the tremendous pain as the bullet wound in his back was re-opened. Then he felt some terrible pounding to his side. When he was able to look up, he saw Tofoya's boot descend time and time again.

The bandit leader had lost the big hat. His black hair whipped about his sweaty face, and the dark eyes seemed double the ordinary size of eyes as he put everything he had into the brutal kicking. His thin lips seemed to disappear into his mouth, so tightly compressed were they at the effort.

The only advantage the situation seemed to offer Cody was that Tofoya had no weapon more deadly than his feet. Even so, a man could submit to only so much pounding. Ignoring the pain from his wound, as well as the deadly pounding, Cody mustered what strength he still possessed and rolled straight at Tofoya's legs. When Tofoya delivered the next kick, Cody grabbed the boot, gave a violent twist, and toppled him.

They came up together and faced each other.

"So you're the gringo who put all the guts into the Indians!" Tofoya snarled in Spanish. "I've been wanting a chance at the one who caused them to stand up against me."

"They didn't get their courage from me, outlaw," Cody replied. "Braver men never fought than the Comanches you faced in that pass."

"It makes no difference now, Texan, because they're all dead. The only thing left is to finish you off."

"Men have died trying to do just that, and I walked away from every one of them. But why stand here talking? Why don't we get at it?"

Tofoya reached for his boot top. When his hand came up, he held a wicked Mexican toothpick.

A gleam of wild hate and of pleasure filled his face and eyes.

Cody reached for the bowie, but his hand grasped an empty sheath. Somehow he had lost the knife in the fight. A wider grin lit Juan Tofoya's face as he faced the unarmed Ranger. Moving in for the kill, he slashed out. Cody's guts would have been emptied on the ground had he not danced back.

Then a shot rang out. But before Cody could wonder about its source, the comanchero chief lay dead on the ground. There was little doubt of that, for the man's once handsome dark face was now a bloody mess. Only the eyes were left, and they stared into a world Cody could not see. He only hoped to avoid the sight for a very, very long time. Only then did he turn to see who had fired the shot.

Mary, rifle still at the ready, met his gaze. She remained silent as they stared into each other's eyes. Then she said, "I think I can claim we're even now. You saved me from him earlier. Now I have done the same for you."

"I was never one to keep score on such things, but I thank you just the same." Cody was silent for a moment, and then he said, "I have just one thing I'd like to ask you."

"What?"

"Why in thunderation did you wait so long?"

She searched for something to say and failed to find it. Then she dropped the rifle and walked to the edge of the lake, where she stood and gazed at the gray cliff above the water. A fish struck somewhere out in the lake, and its splash echoed faintly against the wall of rock. Cody suspected that Mary neither saw nor heard it.

He walked into the trees and returned with the steeldust and the roan.

"Where are you going?" Brad asked.

"I'm going to ride up there with your sister and let her see how Red Wind died. You want to come?"

"No. What will happen to *them*?" Brad indicated the women and children who, slowly and hesitantly, were emerging from the trees.

"I don't know yet," Cody answered. "I don't think they can stay here. They'd be the prey of every outlaw who entered the llano."

"I guess they would," Brad said.

Cody stood a few steps back and watched Mary as she knelt beside the body of Red Wind. His chest was a bloody pulp, and one arm was twisted at an awkward angle. The face was unmarked by violence, however.

Somehow his features appeared more Indian now, or so Cody thought. In death, the cheekbones seemed higher and the face broader. There was now a more pronounced cragginess, as if in death Red Wind had experienced a transition to what he had been in his heart all along. Which was fine, Cody decided, but he wouldn't remember Red Wind as he was now. He would always carry with him the image of Red Wind as he had looked in the ravine the first time they met. Maybe he hadn't been all Comanche then, but he had certainly looked the part.

Stepping forward, Cody took Mary's arm and helped her up. "Come," he said. "We've got some thinking and planning to do."

"Will you help me bury him?" she asked.

"I think we should leave it to what's left of his people. They have their own ways. I think that's what he would want."

Why he felt so, Cody did not know, and he expected an argument from Mary, but none came. From her expression, she now seemed to feel as he did.

Chapter Ten

Cody guessed that they had ridden about twenty miles before he led them into the ravine to make their camp. For their supper they roasted a rabbit and ate it with the corn tortillas that the women of the village had given them. They washed down the food with water from a spring, and it was sweet and cold for desert water.

Sometime later they rolled themselves into their blankets and tried to sleep but couldn't.

"Do you think anything bad will happen to those Indian women and children?" Brad asked Cody.

Cody said, "Wapiti Woman seemed confident. She's an Apache, and she ought to know if her band will take them. Each woman left with ten horses, and Apaches prize horses as much as Comanches always have. There won't be an Apache man in sight who won't be willing to take in a family to get his hands on that many extra mounts."

"Even so, they won't last long," Mary said.

She had been silent since watching the Indian women carry out the Comanche burial ceremony for Red Wind and the other warriors. There was now bitterness in her voice, but Cody thought it an improvement that she was talking again.

"Why do you say that?" he asked, to get her to continue.

"The Apaches are fighting the same fight that the Comanches lost twenty years ago," she said. "That same battle has been fought and lost by Indians across the continent. And there soon won't be any Indians left like the ones we just buried back there."

She didn't speak more, and Cody thought it just as well. She had said all there was to say on the subject.

Silence enfolded the camp again. Crickets chirped their mating calls in the grass about them. A coyote whined in the distance. An owl hooted from a tree in the ravine.

"Cody?"

"Yes, Mary."

"Would it be all right if I went with you and Brad to Mobeetie?"

"Of course it would."

Finally, Cody dropped off to sleep, but not before another thought came to mind...a question, really. What was the solution that Red Wind and Man of Long Legs had dreamed up to save the village once the white man pushed on to the llano? Cody supposed that he would never know, and that was a pity. Such a miracle should not have gone unknown to history.